She didn't back off. On the contrary, she took a step closer, dark blue eyes in his face.

Large, long-lashed, very dark blue eyes that set off an explosion of memory, a flashback to a burst of pain in another time, another place. He stepped back, throwing up his hand in a defensive gesture.

"Mr. Grey?"

It was the burning sting of the nettles brushing against his arm that jolted him back to the doorstep, the present, to the woman who'd disturbed him.

Her free hand was on his arm, steadying him, so close that he caught the sharp scent of fresh herbs, the sweetness of lavender on her clothes, could feel her soft, earthy warmth stirring his numb body to life.

"Lucien?"

Her mouth, soft, pink, inviting, was inches from his own. She was pressed against him, supporting him with her body, and as the stirring became more urgent, more noticeable, her lashes swept down...

He could not have said who moved, only that the gap closed in a hot lightning strike as their lips met in the kind of mindless kiss that sizzled like an electrical overload.

Dear Reader,

I'm so excited about *Redeemed by Her Midsummer Kiss*. It was such fun to return to the villages around Maybridge—Lower Haughton this time, which had a brief mention in *The Bachelor's Baby*, because I needed a river.

I love this world that I've created, based very much on the town and surrounding area where I grew up and is somewhere to the west of London.

Those who know me will not be surprised that *Redeemed by Her Midsummer Kiss* began with a garden. To Honey's reclusive neighbor, frontline newsman Lucien Grey, it appears to be neglected. He doesn't care. He rented the Dower House for its isolation, and he's happy the cottage next door is empty.

To Honey, burned-out after working overseas with a medical-aid charity, it's a place of peace to heal a broken heart.

All would have remained peaceful, except Lucien's contract gardeners were overenthusiastic with the weed killer...

Honey and Lucien have met before on the front line, with bombs falling around them. This time is no less explosive.

I hope you enjoy the garden and how it works its magic to bring these two damaged souls together.

With love,

Liz

Redeemed by Her Midsummer Kiss

Liz Fielding

HARLEQUIN®

Romance™

Recycling programs
for this product may
not exist in your area.

ISBN-13: 978-1-335-40699-6

Redeemed by Her Midsummer Kiss

Copyright © 2022 by Liz Fielding

This edition published by arrangement with Harlequin Books S.A.

For questions and comments about the quality of this book, please contact us at CustomerService@Harlequin.com.

Harlequin Enterprises ULC
22 Adelaide St. West, 41st Floor
Toronto, Ontario M5H 4E3, Canada
www.Harlequin.com

Printed in U.S.A.

Liz Fielding was born with itchy feet. She made it to Zambia before her twenty-first birthday and, gathering her own special hero and a couple of children on the way, lived in Botswana, Kenya and Bahrain—with pauses for sightseeing pretty much everywhere in between. She now lives in the west of England, close to the Regency grandeur of Bath and the ancient mystery of Stonehenge, and these days lets her pen do the traveling.

For news of upcoming books visit Liz's website, lizfielding.com.

Books by Liz Fielding

Harlequin Romance

Christmas at the Harrington Park Hotel

Christmas Reunion in Paris

Destination Brides

A Secret, a Safari, a Second Chance

Summer at Villa Rosa

Her Pregnancy Bombshell

Romantic Getaways

The Sheikh's Convenient Princess

Tempted by Trouble
Flirting with Italian
The Last Woman He'd Ever Date
Vettori's Damsel in Distress
The Billionaire's Convenient Bride

Visit the Author Profile page
at Harlequin.com for more titles.

Redeemed by Her Midsummer Kiss would never have got beyond chapter three without the constant encouragement and support of my wonderful Zoomies, Louise Allen, Lesley Cookman, Janet Gover, Joanna Maitland, Sarah Mallory and Sophie Weston.

I am forever in the debt of the Quayistas, and the champagne is on me when we finally meet up for our much-delayed writing retreat in the Lake District.

Praise for
Liz Fielding

CHAPTER ONE

'With burdocks, hemlock, nettles, cuckoo flowers,
Darnel, and all the weeds that grow.'
—*King Lear*, William Shakespeare

'Murderer!'

Lucien Grey's first reaction to the furious pounding on his front door was to ignore it. After a succession of village worthies, from the vicar to the chair of the parish council, had called to introduce themselves, invite him to open the summer fete or join the bridge, cricket and tennis clubs—all of which he'd politely declined—he'd found a screwdriver and removed the knocker.

And the village had finally got the message. This, however, was not the polite knock of someone hoping to involve him in some local good cause.

The hammering was hard enough to rattle the letterbox.

Concerned that there might have been an accident in the lane, that there might be casualties, he curled his fingers into fists to stop his hands from shaking and forced himself away from his desk. Confronted by a furious female thrusting a fistful of wilting vegetation in his face, it was too late to regret his decision. But he didn't have to stand there and take abuse from some crazy woman.

Wearing dungarees that had seen better days, her white-blonde hair escaping from a knotted scarf, and with pink, overheated cheeks, she looked like someone from a *Dig for Victory* poster circa 1942.

He took a step back, intending to close the door, but she had her boot on the sill faster than the thought could travel from his brain to his hand.

It was a substantial leather boot laced with green twine and, as he stared at it, a lump of dried mud broke off, shattering into dust and clouding the polished surface of the hall floor.

'Who are you?' he demanded. 'What do you want?'

The words were out of his mouth before he could stop them. He didn't care who she was or what she wanted.

Too late.

She was going to tell him. With her foot firmly in the door, there was no escape other than to walk away and leave her in possession of his doorstep. Tempting as the thought was, she was clearly riled enough to follow him inside to continue her verbal battery, so he stood his ground.

'I live in the cottage next door,' she replied, 'And you have sprayed my garden with poison.'

She was tall, but the lack of make-up and shining pinkness of her face made her look like a girl playing dress-up in her great-grandmother's—make that her great-grand*father's*—clothes. Her expression, as murderous as her ridiculous accusation, eyes sparking with fury, suggested otherwise.

'Look at these!'

She shook the dying plants in his face, the bright yellow rubber gloves she wore adding to the bizarre image.

He looked at them then frowned.

'They're nettles.' This madwoman was berating him over nettles? 'Dead nettles.' Clearly not a disgruntled member of the gardening club... 'Whoever sprayed them did you favour, but it wasn't me.'

'Not dead. Dying,' she snapped back. 'Dead nettles are *lamium album*, a valuable nectar source for bumble bees. These are *urtica dioca*, the habitat and food source for red admiral, peacock and small tortoiseshell butterflies.'

'Madam, you may not have noticed, but there are hundreds of nettles—'

'If you look carefully,' she said, cutting him off mid-sentence, 'you will see where the caterpillars have woven silk tents around themselves while they pupate.' She pointed the tip of a grubby, yellow rubber finger at one of the wilted leaves. 'That is a red admiral,' she added. Then, in case he hadn't got the point, '*Would have* been a red admiral if the nettle patch hadn't been sprayed with weed killer.'

'I'm sorry, but if you'd witnessed some of the atrocities that I've seen you wouldn't be weeping over a few butterflies.'

'Sorry?' She looked up from the nettles. 'Such an easy word to say, and rendered meaningless the moment you followed it with "but".'

She was right, of course, but he wasn't about to indulge in semantics with the woman. He just wanted her gone and rescue came from an unexpected source.

'Isn't that a caterpillar?' he asked as he spotted a movement amongst the wilted leaves. 'It looks very much alive to me.'

'What?' She took a closer look. 'Oh my God, it's a small tortoiseshell. There'll be dozens of them.'

'And I have it on good authority that they'll be very hungry.'

She glared at him, not in the least bit amused.

'Very hungry. And you've just wiped out their food source with your chemical attack.'

Lucien felt his blood run ice-cold.

'How dare you?'

'Dare?'

She didn't back off. On the contrary, she took a step closer, dark blue eyes in his face. Large, long-lashed, very dark blue eyes that provoked explosion of memory, a flashback to a burst of pain in another time, another place. He stepped back, throwing up his hand in a defensive gesture.

'Mr Grey?'

It was the burning sting of the nettles brushing against his arm that jolted him back to the doorstep and the present, to the woman who'd disturbed him.

Her free hand was on his arm, steadying him. She was so close that he caught the sharp scent of fresh herbs and the sweetness of lavender on her clothes, could feel her soft, earthy warmth stirring his numb body to life.

'Lucien?'

Her mouth, soft, pink, inviting, was millimetres from his own. She was pressed against him, supporting him with her body. As the stirring became more urgent, more noticeable, her lashes swept down...

He could not have said who moved, only that the gap closed in a hot lightning strike as their lips met in the kind of mindless kiss that sizzled like an electrical overload. *Light the blue touch paper...*

He was somewhere else. The ground was shaking, he was choking, and he knew, just knew, that he had to hold on to this woman, had to save her...

'Mr Grey...' She was holding him and for a moment everything was all right. 'Mr Grey!'

A shiver went through him as he dragged himself back to the silence of a Cotswold village where the only sound was the distant echo of a cuckoo.

'Are you okay?'

The mad nettle woman was regarding him with real concern. He'd just kissed her as if the world was about to end and she was asking him if he was okay? No outrage, no stinging slap…

Could it all have happened in his imagination? The flashbacks came out of the blue, but that was unlike anything he'd ever experienced…

'It's nothing,' he said, taking his cue from her. 'I was stung. My own fault.'

She didn't answer for a moment, those compelling eyes continuing to hold his gaze before dropping to the ugly scar on the inside of his arm, livid against the faded yellow of skin exposed to years of sun. His automatic reaction was to pull away and cover it but she tightened her grip on his arm, preventing him from touching it.

'Don't rub it!' she warned.

'It's nothing,' he repeated. 'An old wound.'

'Yes…'

She continued to hold his arm as if expecting something more but, when he didn't elaborate, she said, 'I was talking about the sting. If you rub the histamine and formic acid into your skin, it will make it much worse. Leave it for ten minutes, then run it under cold water and wash it with soap and water.'

'You don't carry emergency dock leaves?'

He invested the enquiry with all the sarcasm he could muster, desperate to escape, regain his composure and a sense of control. She let her hand drop, leaving behind a smear of dirt from her glove.

'I'm afraid they suffered the same fate as the nettles.'

'I am sorry,' he repeated, and this time he meant it.

He was sorry that he'd left his desk, sorry that he'd opened the door and sorry that he'd chosen Lower Haughton as a bolthole.

The Dower House, part of a great estate, was on the outskirts of the village, isolated but for what, according to the letting agent, had once been the gardener's cottage.

'I was told that the cottage next door was empty,' he said.

'The bees, the butterflies and the insects are always in residence.' She shook her head again, this time impatiently, and a lock of fair hair made a bid for freedom, bouncing over her left eye. She grabbed it with huff of impatience and brushed it behind her ear. 'I would have done the neighbourly thing of calling to introduce myself when I arrived home, but I was warned that you didn't welcome callers.'

'I'm here to work,' he said. 'I don't have time to socialise.'

'I understand, and you have my word that I

won't be knocking on the door to borrow a cup of sugar.'

'There would be no point. I don't use it.'

'Maybe you should give it a try.' Her mouth twitched, and for a moment he thought there might be a smile to take the sting out of her words, but she managed to restrain herself. 'It has a very dodgy history, and isn't great for your health, but it beats the hell out of weed killer.'

'From what I've seen of your garden, madam, weed killer should be at the top of your shopping list.'

'Excuse me?'

'You have to admit that your garden is a bit…'

Realising that he was being drawn into a conversation he hadn't asked for, didn't want, he stopped.

'A bit…?' she prompted and, when he refused to be tempted, a hint of a victory smile drew his gaze back to her mouth.

Sweet, yielding, tasting of strawberries…

'The word you're struggling for, Mr Grey, is *wild*,' she said, snapping him back to reality.

'Are you telling me that it's deliberate?'

She might smell like heaven and have come-to-bed eyes but she was a crazy woman who had the dress sense of a navvy and actively encouraged weeds.

She almost certainly had cats.

'And how does the rest of the village feel about

that?' he asked. 'Because, when I arrived in Lower Haughton, I noticed a sign boasting that it had won a gold medal in the Best Kept Village competition last year. They didn't win that with weeds.'

'You'd be surprised.'

'Only if I gave a damn,' he said, determined to put an end this conversation. 'I don't know what happened to your nettles, but I will find out, and I'll make sure it doesn't happen again.'

He made a move to close the door, but the boot stayed put.

'I know exactly what happened,' she said, and clearly had no intention of moving until she'd shared the bad news. 'You've hired a couple of cowboys who cut the grass too short and whose answer to everything else—bugs or weeds—involved chemicals.'

'I've hired no one. The lease includes garden and cleaning services. The men who were here this morning were just doing their job.'

'Then it wasn't carelessness?' She was very still now. 'It was deliberate,' she pressed. 'A contract killing.'

'No!' The last thing he'd wanted was a chat with the garden crew. They'd called out to him about the weeds when he'd come back from his run, and he'd told them to do whatever they thought best. Finding himself on the defensive, he said, 'You can't deny that your garden is overrun with weeds which, according to the contractors, are encroaching on mine.'

'What constitutes a weed depends on your point of view, Mr Grey. Unlike your sterile acre, my great-aunt turned her garden into a wildlife haven, and I intend to keep her legacy alive.'

A wildlife haven?

The cottage backed onto the river where he forced himself to run every morning. A glimpse of thatch beyond what, in the days when it had been part of the Hartford estate, must have been a well-kept orchard. The trees were thick with blossom, but the grass and weeds grew thick and high with neglect. He'd been told that the cottage was empty.

Not any more, apparently, but how she kept her property was none of his business and he held up his hands in a gesture of surrender.

'I'd offer to buy you replacement nettles, but I doubt the local nursery would be able to supply them.'

'Not intentionally,' she agreed, an idea that appeared to amuse her. 'Don't worry about speaking to your so-called gardeners. I'll make sure that they don't repeat their offence.'

She finally stepped back but, free to shut the door and go back to his desk, he found himself reluctant to do either.

'Will you be able to save them?' he asked. 'The caterpillars?'

But, now that he was the one who wanted to talk, she was the one backing away. 'I'll do my best.'

And then she turned and strode away down the drive. Lucien stood for a moment, watching as her long legs covered the ground so fast that she was almost out of sight when he called after her.

'There are plenty of nettles on the path by the river.'

Stupid. She must know that. But she didn't hear. Or maybe she did, but she didn't look back, and a moment later she was out of sight, leaving him with only a powdering of dry mud on his hall floor and a burning itch in his arm to show that she'd been there.

His hand hovered over his arm as the urge to rub it intensified.

Don't touch it for ten minutes?

Really? It was that specific? Or was that the length of time she wanted him to suffer?

On the other hand, she'd sounded as if she knew what she was talking about. With a garden over-grown with nettles, she had probably learned the hard way.

Honey was practically running by the time she reached the ancient oak near the gate of Lucien Grey's hideaway. Out of sight of the house, she leaned against its trunk to catch her breath.

She couldn't believe that she'd called the hero

of Bouba al-Asad a murderer. Lectured him like a schoolboy.

Now that the rush of adrenaline-fuelled anger had receded, she felt a rush of shame. The man who had once courted danger in his flak jacket and helmet, veteran of a thousand reports to camera while under fire in the world's trouble spots, had the gaunt, hollowed-out look of a man who'd seen too much.

He was not the tanned, vigorous man whose shrapnel wound she had cleaned and dressed in a makeshift hospital while he'd continued to talk into the camera. She'd told him that he needed to be medevacked for proper attention, irritable that he'd been taking up her time when, unlike her other patients, he had a choice about being there.

Catching her tone, he'd looked back, and there had been a moment when he'd actually looked at her. Not just as some faceless person who'd patched him up, but really looked at her, as if searching for the person behind the mask and the disposable gloves.

He'd taken a step towards her as if to say something but, at that moment, an explosion had shaken the temporary hospital, filling the air with choking dust, and she'd had her hands full with the evacuation of the wounded.

By the time she'd had a moment to catch her breath, to think about him, he was gone.

She'd been astonished when she'd come home

to discover that they were neighbours. The gossip in the village shop was that he had leased the Dower House in order to write a book about his experiences, but the excitement at having a celebrity amongst them had been swiftly quelled.

He was polite, she'd been told, but invitations to dinner, to give a talk to the WI and to open the village fete had been declined due to the pressure of a tight deadline, and she hadn't called to introduce herself and remind him that they'd met.

It should have been galling that he hadn't recognised her. But, after ranting at him like a fishwife, she was grateful that she'd been wearing a mask the first time and that he'd been too distracted to notice her, but for a rare moment of connection that had never left her. That for a split second had been there today...

According to Alma Lacey, who cleaned, shopped and cooked for him, he spent all his time locked away in his study—a room she had been forbidden to touch—and she rarely saw him.

Maybe he was working long hours, but that was more than screen pallor. A close-clipped beard did nothing to disguise the way the skin was stretched over the fine bones of his face. There was a glint of silver in the familiar thick mass of dark curls, and when she'd stepped up to face him she could feel him trembling.

He'd been angry but he hadn't been seeing her. He'd gone to some much darker place inside his head, and in a heartbeat she had been support-ing him as the terror had gripped him, as it had morphed into raw need. A need that had found a shocking echo deep in her belly.

She knew that emptiness, that desperation. Feeling his unmistakable response to her close-ness, she'd wanted the mindless oblivion of phys-ical connection, and for a moment she'd been a little lost herself.

A shudder passed through her—an awareness that all it would have taken was a touch and they would have been ripping each other's clothes off right there on the doorstep.

Lucien Grey had been something of media heartthrob, a reason to switch on the evening news, and no one would blame her for grabbing a moment of meaningless lust.

No one but her.

He bore scars that went much deeper than the one on his arm. Invisible scars that were carried by men and women returning from the front line, having lost friends and having seen things that were burned for ever into their brain.

She knew enough, bore her own roster of mental scars, to understand that he'd had no idea where he was in that moment, no idea what he was doing. It had happened to her when she'd caught the chemical stench of the weed killer and it had felt as if the war had followed her home.

She would have to apologise, and under normal

circumstances that would have had to be done face to face. Not this time.

While he really needed to get out and talk to people, he wouldn't want to see her again. She'd leave a note, a pot of honey and some early strawberries from the garden on his back porch where Alma Lacey would find them and take them in.

But not before she'd rehomed the infant caterpillars on the nettles on the towpath and done what she could for the red admiral larvae and the tortoiseshell eggs.

What she should have done instead of storming next door with her accusation of lepidopteral homicide.

CHAPTER TWO

'To be ignorant of what occurred before you were born is to remain perpetually a child. For what is the worth of a human life unless it is woven into the life of our ancestors by the records of history?'
—Marcus Tullius Cicero

LUCIEN SHUT THE door and leaned back against it, rubbing his face hard with his hands in an effort to clear his head. Wipe away the disturbing encounter.

That was the most he'd spoken to anyone in the weeks since he'd been back in England, but her anger had made it easier. He hadn't stopped to think, he'd just reacted, but it had not been his finest moment, even if she had just called him a murderer.

And then there was a look that had sent him reeling back into the darkness. The choking dust, the certainty that he had to save her: where had that come from?

And that kiss…

Had that been real or part of the flashback? It had never happened before, and he could taste strawberries… Or had that been the smell of them on her lips?

He didn't even know her name and she'd been mad enough about the nettles. If he'd kissed her, she would certainly have beaten him with them, and with every justification.

He needed to get a grip, get back to work, but first he'd ask the housekeeper for the woman's name and write a note, apologising for his rudeness. And the damn nettles. He'd better email the letting agency too, to explain what had happened and ensure that her precious wilderness wasn't violated again. He could only hope that she'd keep her promise not to bother him.

Except that he was already bothered. He could still see her mouth within kissing distance of his own. Feel every point where her body had touched his: her hand on his arm, his shoulder. Her breasts against his chest. Her hip, her thigh…

And those eyes.

One minute they'd been flashing with anger, then something unreadable that had tapped into a fleeting memory, leaving him with a disturbing sense of *déjà vu*.

As if he could have forgotten meeting a woman with that much passion. He swore, turning to look out of one of the tall windows on either side of the front door, seeking a distraction from the fear that his brain was turning to mush.

He'd barely noticed the garden when he'd arrived and hadn't left the house since. His mother used to talk wistfully about the garden she'd had as a child and, little more than a child himself, he'd told her that one day he'd buy her a cottage in the country.

These days he owned a London flat that overlooked the Thames. It wasn't a home, just an investment sourced by his accountant when he'd been a thousand miles away. If he'd been there, he'd have been safe from annoying neighbours and their nettles. But the same careful accountant had arranged for it to be let while he'd been on an overseas assignment and he hadn't anticipated returning until early next year.

He turned as sounds from the kitchen warned him that Mrs Lacey had arrived. He did his best to stay out of her way, communicating via notes stuck to the fridge with a magnet. However, there were some things you could not put off, and an apology was one of them.

She was stocking the fridge and nearly dropped a pot of yogurt when he walked into the kitchen.

'Mr Grey, you startled me... Is there something I can get you?'

'No... That is, yes. I need the name of the woman who lives in the cottage next door.'

He didn't doubt that she knew it. Lower Haughton was that kind of place.

'Do you mean Honeysuckle?'

'Is that what it's called? Honeysuckle Cottage?'

'What? Oh, no. The cottage is Orchard End.

Honeysuckle lives there. She inherited from her great-aunt a few months ago.'

'Honeysuckle?' Anyone less like a flower would be hard to imagine. 'Her name is Honeysuckle?'

Mrs Lacey smiled. 'Honeysuckle Rose. So sweet.'

That wasn't the word he would have chosen. Passionate, angry, alive... He tightened his hand into a fist, desperate to drive away the thought.

'Has she been here?' Mrs Lacey asked.

'She has. Apparently the garden people sprayed weed killer on her nettles.'

'Oh, dear. She won't have been happy about that.'

A prime example of English understatement.

According to Honeysuckle, he was a murderer, a contract killer, a purveyor of chemical warfare...

Images flashed through his mind of a reality she couldn't begin to imagine. The next thing he knew, he was sitting at the kitchen table and Mrs Lacey was placing a cup of tea in front of him.

'I've put some sugar in it. I know you don't normally take it, but you look as if you could do with it,' she said.

'Miss Rose said much the same thing.'

Was she *Miss* Rose?

Mrs Lacey didn't suggest otherwise. 'If that's what Honey said, Mr Grey, you should listen. Her family are a bit of a legend around here.'

He sipped the tea despite the sugar and she was right. It helped.

'A legend? In what way?'

'Well, Jack Rose went to China with Lord Hartford back in the nineteenth century. They brought back all sorts of plants no one had ever seen before. And James Rose was championing organic gardening when everyone else was rushing to chemicals.'

'I see.'

'James's daughter, Flora Rose, was Honey's great-aunt. Her passion was for re-wilding the countryside,' she continued. 'It's thanks to her that we have so many wildflowers and butterflies in the village.' And presumably nettles, he thought. 'They bring in the visitors.'

'The letting agent mentioned that the owner was abroad.'

'Honey flew home when Flora was taken poorly just before Christmas. Not in time, sadly.' She shook her head. 'The poor girl was in bits about that, but Flora didn't want her worried. In the end we decided to call and tell her that she needed to come home. I just wish we'd done it sooner.'

'She stayed on when she inherited the cottage?'

'No. She went back to work straight after the funeral, but she's home now. We're all hoping that she'll stay. There's always been a Rose at Orchard End but there's not a lot to keep a young woman in the village these days.'

'No. Well, thank you for the information. I'm sorry to have disturbed you while you're working. I'll take this upstairs with me.'

'It's a lovely day out there, Mr Grey. You should bring your laptop down and work in the garden. If you go down by the boat house you might see—'

'Boat house? No one mentioned a boat house.' Or maybe they had. He hadn't paid much attention to the details.

'It's through the copse. Towards the big house. You wouldn't find it unless you were looking for it. No one will disturb you down there.'

Too late, Lucien thought.

He was already disturbed and would remain so until he'd apologised to his butterfly-loving neighbour. Once he'd done that, he would be able to put her out of his mind.

'It's a lovely spot. When I get back, I'll clean it out for you,' Mrs Lacey added when he didn't answer.

'Thank you,' he said, responding on automatic, then belatedly catching what the woman had said. 'Back? Are you going away?'

'It's my brother and sister-in-law's golden wedding anniversary this weekend. Jane and I started school on the same day and we've been best friends ever since. I met Mr Lacey when I was one of her bridesmaids. It'll be our golden next year.'

He managed a smile. 'Congratulations. Will you be away long?'

'We're driving over this afternoon so that I can help Jane get ready for the party, and then the four of us are going to spend a couple of weeks in a villa we've rented in Spain.'

Lucien had done everything he could to avoid Mrs Lacey in the months since he'd arrived at the Dower House, but her absence would leave a huge gap.

'The agency has arranged for someone else to come in while I'm away,' she assured him. 'Sarah doesn't cook, but I've filled your freezer. It's all labelled. I've stuck a list to the top of the freezer. Just take out what you want in the morning and follow the instructions on the lid. You won't know I'm gone.'

'You underestimate yourself, Mrs Lacey.' She had been unfailingly considerate, un-intrusive and, if he wasn't eating much, it had nothing to do with her cooking. 'I hope you have a wonderful time.'

The river that flowed at the bottom of the Orchard End garden wasn't grand. No more than twenty metres across, the Hart was little more than a stream, but it was sparkling in the morning light as Honey walked along the path. She planned to leave her peace offering in the back porch of the Dower House.

She hadn't walked this way since she'd come home, and was drawn by the glimpse of pink amongst the grass that could only be fritillaries. Having taken a photograph with her phone, she looked around. The trout were rising to snap at thousands of mayflies that had just hatched, a sign that the river was in good shape.

The same couldn't be said of the old boat house.

It was a substantial, two-storey timber building that had once been a pretty pale blue, the windows and balcony on the upper floor painted white. Now the faded paint was peeling off in strips and the glass in a couple of the windows was cracked. Shocked by the decay, she climbed the steps to the wide deck to take a better look.

There had been punts, rowing boats and a sleek slipper launch when she'd been a child but, through one of the cracked and filthy panes, she could see that the wet dock was empty. There was only an old punt, falling to pieces, its cushions shredded by mice, lying at the back.

She wondered if the present Lord Hartford—who'd handed the whole lot to an agent to manage, preferring to live in the south of France—hoped the same fate would befall the boat house.

Like Hartford Manor and the Dower House, it had been listed as a building of historical interest and could not be demolished without permission. But restoring it to its original status as a luxurious playhouse for the rich and entitled, under the watchful eye of Historic England and local planning authority would cost a great deal of money.

The only alternative was to let it rot until, eventually, it fell down. A sad ending that wouldn't matter much to anyone but for the fact that Lower Haughton was in a narrow valley. Should the boat house collapse into the river during one of the storms that were becoming increasingly common, the water would rapidly back up.

The Manor and Dower House were not in any danger, and the cottage was far enough back to be safe, but the village would be flooded…

'Miss Rose. To what new disaster do I owe this pleasure?'

Honey, absorbed in visualising exactly how flooding would play out—the evacuation of the cottages, the inundation of the shops on the lower part of the village—jumped half out of her skin.

'It hasn't happened yet,' she replied, spinning round to face Lucien Grey.

Too fast.

The world lurched a little and she threw out a hand to keep her balance. For a moment she had it, but then there was a crack as the board on which she was standing yielded to the sudden movement, and there was a shocked, slow-motion moment as her right foot disappeared through the deck.

Flailing wildly now, she lost her grip on the basket and strawberries rolled across the deck like blood spatter. Then there was a jolt through her entire body as her foot hit loose gravel and began to slide forward.

At that point she lost her fight with gravity and went down backwards in a bone-shaking fall. Her shoulders hit first, then her head whipped back and thumped against the deck. Winded, she thought it was over, but the weight of her body carried her forward on the gravel until her foot caught on something. She gasped with pain as it was wrenched sideways and her sandal fell off, probably never to be seen again.

For a moment she thought that was it, but then something jagged drove into her foot. She would have screamed if she'd had the breath. Warned Lucien Grey to stay back. But the deck shook beneath her, intensifying the pain, as he leapt to her rescue. He'd be no help if he ended up in the same position, but he was the one who was yelling, 'Don't move!' as he knelt beside her.

She closed her eyes, heard three urgent beeps as he dialled 999 and a moment later said, 'Ambulance.' There was a momentary pause. 'Oh, yes,' he said with a sigh that might have been regret, 'She's certainly breathing, but she's had a fall and hit her head…'

It's my foot!

'And she might have hurt her leg.'

Foot, foot, foot…

'Conscious?'

She opened her eyes.

'Yes, she's conscious. How old?' He looked at her for an answer, but she was shivering, light-headed… 'She dresses early nineteen-forties allotment, but I'd say she's about thirty.'

I'm wearing crops and my favourite linen shirt, and I'm twenty-nine…

'No, I won't move her.' He gave his address. 'Tell the crew to drive around to the back of the house and cut across the grass, then follow the footpath through the wood to the boat house.'

Having given the despatcher directions for the crew to find them, he took off his sweater, knelt down and tucked it around her, comfortingly warm from his body.

'They won't be long,' he said.

His hand lingered for a moment on her shoulder but, before she could summon up the breath to thank him, he stood up and walked away, each step causing a minute, agonising jar that seemed to go through every cell.

'Be careful…' Her mouth moved, but no sound emerged.

For heaven's sake…

She dragged in some air and tried again, this time with more success, but there was no answer.

Had he gone to meet the ambulance? Gone to direct them to where she was lying before getting on with whatever kept him so busy at the Dower House?

What had she expected when she'd called him a murderer? Accused him of chemical warfare…?

Under the circumstances she should be grateful that he hadn't walked away and left her lying there. Grateful at the swiftness of his reaction, even if his description of her had been less than flattering.

She didn't need or want his flattery.

A hand to hold onto right now would be good, though. She had to clamp her lips tight against the temptation to call out and beg him to stay with her until the paramedics arrived.

Twenty minutes, she told herself. It would take twenty minutes for an ambulance to arrive from Maybridge. She needed to concentrate on relaxing her muscles and breathing through the pain. Concentrate on the scent of his sweater—fabric softener and leather where his back had rubbed against his chair. Something more personal. His soap, maybe…was that sandalwood?

Her attempt to identify the elusive scent was shattered by a hideous screeching sound. Muscles that she'd worked hard to relax immediately tensed and this time, as the pain ripped through her, she had enough breath to let the world know how it felt, letting out a long, agonised, 'Owww!'

'Hang on, I'll be right back.'

She remained very still for a moment, barely breathing until the pain subsided a little, just grateful that he was still within shouting distance.

She looked in the direction his voice had come from. There was no sign of Lucien Grey, but the boat house door, having been dragged on rusty hinges, stood open.

'This is so not the moment for exploring,' she muttered, but without conviction as, clammy and dizzy, she closed her eyes.

When she opened them, he was kneeling beside her, his hand on her forehead.

'You look terrible. Did you faint?'

'My blood pressure dropped.'

'You fainted.'

'Smartarse,' she muttered then, noticed that he was holding a hammer. 'Are you going to finish me off?'

He responded with a huff that wasn't quite a laugh, muttered something that might have been, 'Don't tempt me,' and removed his hand, leaving a chill where it had been.

'You had me worried for a moment,' he said, turning his attention to the boards above her leg, 'but your tongue is as sharp as ever.'

'I'm sorry about that but I'm having a bit of a bad morning.'

'For which you have no one but yourself to blame. I'm sure I don't need to remind you that you promised not to bother me again.'

'I'm not bothering you!'

He glanced at her. 'This is not bothering me?'

'No. Yes… I was going to the village to post a birthday card.'

'The village is in the opposite direction,' he pointed out.

'There's a public footpath through your woods, and I thought, why not take the scenic route and leave some strawberries and a pot of honey on your back porch? Something to sweeten you up.'

'I got the message. No need to hammer it home.'

'And then I noticed the fritillaries,' she continued, determined to finish.

'Fritillaries?'

'Do you have to repeat everything I say?' She would have shaken her head at his ignorance, but it hurt too much. 'Those pink flowers over there. Bees love them,' she added, but he didn't look. 'That was when I saw the state of the boat house.'

'And why would you care?'

'I'm a concerned citizen?' she managed, through teeth gritted against the pain.

'You are trespassing, Miss Rose. Causing even more damage.'

'Don't be such an ass, Mr Grey…' She'd gone for brisk but didn't make it much above a whisper. 'There's water…in my basket…' He raised an eyebrow.

'Is that wise?'

'My blood pressure…'

CHAPTER THREE

*'Here's Thyme to give you courage and Rose-
mary for the past, Sweet Lavender for a loyal
heart and Rose, a love to last; Sage for a life
that is long and brave, Mint to quicken the
brain, Violets to ward off evil ones and Basil to
cure the pain.'*
—R B Lytton

LUCIEN GREY SET the basket straight and handed her
the bottle of water without comment, but Honey's
hand was shaking so much that she couldn't flip
the spout.

He took it from her, opened it and then placed a
hand beneath her neck to support her. Those long,
cool fingers tangling in her hair were better than
any painkiller but, afraid he was going to lift her
head, she squeaked out a warning. 'No!'

'You think you've a back injury?' he asked.

She made a quick tour of her body, flexing muscles. 'No. Whiplash, probably...'

He nodded but didn't take his hand away as he
placed the bottle to her lips. As she was flat on
her back, most of it ran down her face and neck.

'Have you had enough?' he asked when she
stopped to catch her breath.

'Yes...'

'Tell me if you want more.'

He put the bottle down, then undid all his good work by catching his watch strap in her hair.

She might have overdone the scream.

He muttered an expletive as he disentangled it. 'Sorry…'

She wasn't sure if he was apologising for swearing or for the hair but, heart hammering, she reminded herself that he was trying to help.

'It's okay… Ripping out my hair made me forget all about my foot.'

'So not all bad news, then.'

'My foot is the bad news,' she muttered, but he was now fully focussed on the boards that needed moving, testing the wood with his fingers.

'The wood is really soft here,' he said, looking up to where she could see the damage to the balcony, where water must have been coming through for years. 'You're lucky it's just your foot that went through.'

'I'm glad you think so,' she said, but he was already working at the spongy wood with the claw end of the hammer. 'You do realise that you're tearing apart a listed building?' she continued, more to keep herself focussed on something other than the pain than because she cared.

He tore up a sizeable chunk of the deck and threw it to one side. 'It's just an old boat house.'

'The operative word is "old". It has history.'

'It's an old and rotting boat house,' he said,

moving on to the next plank. 'A health and safety nightmare that should be pulled down before it falls down.'

'I refer you to the word "listed". Pulling it down would get the owner into all sorts of trouble.'

That finally got his attention. 'You were serious? I know the house is listed, but what's so special about the boat house?'

'It was designed by some famous nineteenth-century architect who was a friend of the Hartfords. Their weekend parties were—' she dug her nails into her palms as a wave of pain hit her '—legendary.'

'There's a lot of that about,' he said.

'What?'

The word came out as little more than a squeak and he stopped what he was doing.

'Is there anything I can do?'

'Just get on with that,' she said through gritted teeth.

'I've heard that there's a legendary family of gardeners,' he prompted as he tore up another piece of the deck.

'Oh?' Alma had been talking. Which meant that he'd been asking… 'Maybe "notorious" is a better word for the boat house,' she said. 'Rumour has it that the titled and the famous used it to indulge in all kinds of extra-marital shenanigans. I've been told that the bedroom has a mirrored ceiling.'

'Only told?' He'd got to a point where the wood was still in good condition, and it splintered as he levered it up. 'Are you telling me that you haven't been up there to check it out?'

'The Hartford family were still in residence at the Manor when I left home. Trespassers were discouraged.'

'I'll go along with that.'

'It's probably just lurid gossip,' she continued, ignoring his interruption. 'About the mirror. The rest is true enough. Aunt Flora once saw the Prince of Wales swimming naked in front of the cottage.'

'What a pity she didn't have a camera with her. The tabloids would have paid well for that picture.'

'What? No! It was the one who abdicated. He was with Mrs Simpson, and she was naked too, but a photograph wouldn't have done Flora any good. The newspapers had been gagged.'

He stopped what he was doing and looked at her. 'You're talking about the mid-nineteen-thirties. How old was your aunt?'

'At the time? She must have been about ten. Her father had a word with his lordship and after that the guests stayed downstream.'

'I'm surprised they were bothered.'

'My great-great-grandfather was not a man to be trifled with.'

'He was one of the gardening legends?'

'Yes.' She swallowed. How long had it been since he'd called the ambulance? 'The previous Prince of Wales—King Edward the VII,' she added, to make sure he knew who she was talking about '—was a frequent visitor with his mistresses too. And in the sixties, there were parties with rock stars, designers, artists… Princess Margaret was a regular—'

'Hello?' A tall figure in a green paramedic uniform appeared by the deck. 'What's happened here?'

'I put my foot through a rotting board, went down hard on my back and hit my head,' Honey said before Lucien could put in his pennyworth.

The man turned to him anyway. 'Did you see it happen, sir?'

'Yes. I think it's just the one weak spot, but test before you put your weight on it. And don't slip on the strawberries.'

'Thank you, sir.' The man stepped carefully onto the deck, checking the board would take his weight before he moved on, then knelt down beside her. 'Hello, miss, I'm Raj, and this is my partner Jools. What would you like me to call you?'

Honey had had a lifetime of that moment of disbelief when people heard her name for the first time, but they'd need all her details, so she braced herself.

'My name is Honeysuckle Rose.'

The paramedic glanced at Lucien to check just how hard that the bang on her head had been.

'Rose is her surname,' he confirmed.

'Most people take the short option and call me Honey,' she said.

'Right then, Honey. Jools will take your blood pressure while I take some details. Do you live here?'

'No,' she said, quickly, holding out her arm for Jools to attach a cuff and fix a pulse oximeter to her finger. 'I live next door at Orchard End. I was on my way to deliver strawberries and a pot of honey from my aunt's bees… My bees…'

She was talking too much…

Jools took her temperature while Raj began to rattle through the standard questions: date of birth, medical history, allergies.

'Do you live alone, Honey?'

'Yes.'

Lucien raised an eyebrow. 'Really? No cats?'

She didn't miss the implication that she was a crazy cat lady who grew weeds and in the seventeenth century would probably have been ducked in the village pond as a witch.

'Raj isn't interested in four-footed companions, Mr Grey. He's concerned about how I'm going to manage.'

'Let's worry about that when we know the worst,' Jools said quickly, sensing an edge to the exchange. 'Can you tell us exactly what happened, Honey?'

She repeated what she'd said, then added, 'My foot caught on something as I went down, so there's a sprain. And I appear to have speared it on something. A nail, possibly. Or a piece of wood.'

Lucien muttered an expletive. 'Why the hell didn't you say?'

'You've seen enough first aid to know that there is nothing you could have done except remove the boards. Which you've done.' She turned back to Jools. 'And I've almost certainly got whiplash.'

Raj smiled. 'You seem to know what you're talking about, Honey.'

'I'm a nurse, Raj.'

'Oh. Right.' He frowned. 'I haven't seen you at Maybridge General.'

'I trained in London.'

'That's a bit of a long commute,' he said, taking a torch from the bag and peering beneath the deck.

'What have we got?' Jools asked.

'It looks like a piece of wood has broken off one of the piles holding up the deck. It's embedded in her heel. We need to get her out of here...'

They checked to make sure that there were no back injuries and then, using a backboard, lifted her out.

Lucien swore as he saw the long, jagged splinter of wood that was embedded in her foot.

'Are you going to leave it there?' he demanded.

'That's best left for the hospital to deal with, Mr Grey. Will you be coming with us in the ambulance?'

'No!' Honey said before he did. 'That's not necessary.'

Three hours later Honey, with her foot cleaned, stitched and booted in a brace to support the sprain, her neck in a collar, and clutching a bag containing a shedload of pills, dressings and holding a pair of crutches, was wheeled to the front entrance of the hospital.

'Shall I take you over to the phone so that you can call a taxi?' the porter asked.

'That won't be necessary.'

Honey's heart did a little up and down flutter as her reluctant neighbour lowered the newspaper he was reading and rose to his feet.

The up was relief. Her purse, along with her phone, was in her basket, which was probably still on the boat house deck. She'd thought she would have to call and ask Alma or Brian to pick her up.

The down was guilt.

Lucien Grey had been stuck here for hours waiting for her, all because she'd been side-tracked by a glimpse of fritillaries.

'Mr Grey… I didn't expect you to follow me. To wait for me.'

'I realise that you have a very low opinion of me, Miss Rose—'

'No!'

The man was a hero. Front line reporters and photographers were supposed to keep their distance, report dispassionately, but while everyone else had been running for cover he'd risked his life digging a family out of their bombed home in the middle of a rocket attack.

His eyebrows rose in way that suggested he was not convinced by her denial.

'Really,' she insisted.

He shrugged. 'You may have forgotten your promise to stay away from my front door…'

'I was going to your back door,' she objected, 'And I wasn't going to knock. I was just going to leave the honey and strawberries with a note apologising for the way I spoke to you yesterday. On the bench. In the porch.'

'What a pity you didn't stick to the plan,' he muttered, folding the newspaper and handing it to someone who was patiently waiting for a loved one.

'When I saw the state…' She stopped. He didn't care about the boat house. Why would he? 'You're right. I should have posted the note and given the strawberries and honey to someone who deserved them.'

'I agree, but the accident happened in my garden. And, since you had neither purse nor phone with you to call for assistance, I had little choice but to deliver them.'

Begrudging, but he'd made the effort, and that was what counted.

'I'm sorry you were put to so much trouble, but thank you. If you hand them over, I'll call a cab.'

'Don't be ridiculous. I'll drive you home.'

The porter, who'd been watching this exchange with interest, said, 'Excuse me, Mr Grey, but I just want to say what an honour...' He stopped at her touch and read her warning look. 'Well, I'm sure you've heard it all before. Let's get you on your feet, Honey, and you can be on your way.'

'Thank you,' she murmured to him as he settled her on her crutches.

He nodded. 'You take care now,' he said. 'Both of you.'

He whirled away the wheelchair before she could answer, and she turned reluctantly to face Lucien, who had retrieved her basket from beneath his seat.

'It was very kind of you to come and pass on my things. I really am sorry you've had such a long wait when I know that you're working on your book.'

'I've passed the time looking up fritillaries, nettles and some of the gossip about Hartford Manor on my phone,' he said.

'Oh? Did you learn anything useful?'

'That fritillaries like damp meadows, that you can make rope from nettles and that I have a very low tolerance of hospital waiting rooms.'

He relieved her of the bag containing antibiotics and painkillers, dropping them into her basket and leaving her with both hands free. It was, however, noticeable that he kept a safe distance between them as she carefully swung herself in the direction of the door.

Very wise.

The way things were going, she'd probably trip him up and lay him out cold on the waiting room floor.

It might even be an accident.

'So?' he asked. 'What's the damage?'

'A sprain and a foot packed with antibiotics.'

'Which means?'

'Ice packs at regular intervals, keeping my foot up as much as possible and time.'

'Those butterflies have got a lot to answer for.'

'Don't blame the butterflies!' she shot back, finally snapping. 'They're the victims here.' Honey's head was suddenly splitting, and she felt clammy. 'Can we get a move on? It's hot in here and I need some fresh air.'

Lucien took a sideways glance at her. Honeysuckle—such a ridiculous name—was much too pale and she was undoubtedly in pain.

All his instincts demanded that he offer her support, but he was rather afraid that her response would be to hit him with a crutch.

No doubt he deserved it.

He didn't want to be here, but he'd had a choice. She hadn't. Clearly, he was the last person she'd have asked for help, but when he'd picked up the honey to return it to the basket he'd discovered her purse and phone, and it had been too late to catch the ambulance.

And that, he told himself, was the only reason he'd followed her to the hospital. So that she would be able to call for help or pay for a taxi.

Of course, by the time he'd arrived, she'd been whisked away to have an X-ray and he'd had no choice but to wait.

Afraid he'd miss her if he went for a walk in the hospital grounds, he'd bought a sandwich and a newspaper to hide behind.

He'd read it from end to end and done both crosswords before she had finally appeared. A time-wasting nuisance, but there was no denying that he had been partly responsible for her accident. He had no excuse for the way he'd spoken to her, yesterday or today.

He hadn't seen her note, but she would discover his in the letterbox by her gate when she got home, and hopefully accept that he wasn't entirely without manners.

Or pity.

There was a bench not far from the front door which, from the litter on the ground, and the smell, was clearly there for the benefit of smokers. At that moment it was unoccupied.

'It's a bit of a trek to the car,' he said. 'Why don't you wait here, and I'll bring it to the door?'

'It's a no-parking area.'

'It's a pick up, not parking—and to be frank, Miss Rose, you don't look that hot.'

'I wasn't actually aiming for hot. But I left my lipstick in my basket—'

'Dammit! That wasn't…' He stopped. She was in pain and he was being a jerk. 'Do you need your water bottle?'

'No.' Then, making a effort to be polite in the face of his irritation, 'Thank you. I just want to get home and have a cup of tea.' She found a smile from somewhere. It wasn't the real thing, but it was a brave effort. 'Since you feel so bad, I'll let you make it.'

Damn the woman. She didn't give an inch. But he was fighting down a smile of his own as he headed for the car park.

CHAPTER FOUR

'...dandelion wine is summer in a glass.
Rich, golden and warming...'
—Anonymous

IF SHE'D THOUGHT about it, Honey would have expected a famous and well-heeled bachelor to drive a sleek, fast two-seater. Or maybe one of those dashing sports cars that looked like something out of a wartime movie would have suited him better.

In both instances she would have been wrong. Lucien Grey was driving a four-wheel drive. Not a glossy new one, the kind with a fridge in the boot for picnics, but one that had been around the block more times than it could count. And might have run into it a time or two.

'Whoever sold you that saw you coming,' she said.

'A friend who finds sheep more relaxing than shell fire loaned it to me.'

Honey swallowed. She was feeling better after a few minutes in the fresh air and had no excuse for her snippiness. There was just something about Lucien Grey. It had been there in the heat of a hospital tent set up in a refugee camp. It had been there yesterday on his doorstep.

If she were a cat, she'd say he was rubbing her

fur the wrong way. Which was ridiculous. She wasn't a cat, and he wasn't stroking her, although the idea was a lot more appealing that it should be. The memory of that kiss had left an undeniable impression. The taste of him had lingered all the while she'd been rehoming the caterpillars. And when he'd draped his sweater over her, laid cool fingers against her neck…

'Well,' she said with sham brightness, 'that was very kind of him.'

'Her. Jenny Logan?'

'Oh…yes.' She was one of the few women reporting from trouble spots. 'Sheep?'

'The last I saw of her she was up to her neck in newborn lambs with a film crew in tow.'

'A film crew?'

'Are you going to repeat everything I say?'

'I'm sorry,' she said. 'It must be infectious.'

'You are…'

She tilted her head to one side…or would have done if the collar hadn't been holding her neck rigid.

'I am?'

'Causing an obstruction.'

'I told you this was a no-parking area,' she reminded him, handing him her crutches. Then, realising just how high it was, she looked for something to hang onto so that she could pull herself up into the seat.

There was nothing.

The kind of people who drove around in four-by-fours were, it seemed, expected to be fit enough to climb aboard under their own steam.

'This isn't going to work,' she said. 'Give me my basket and I'll call a taxi.'

'Don't be ridiculous.' He put the basket and the crutches on the back seat, then turned to her. 'Put your arms around my neck and I'll lift you in.'

'What? No!' she protested. 'I may have a flower fairy name but I'm a fully grown woman. You'll throw your back out.'

'Leave me to worry about my back and just do as you're told.'

'Excuse me?'

'We're blocking the hospital entrance. Close your eyes and think of your weeds if getting that close to me bothers you. I promise it will be over in a minute.'

As if to confirm what he was saying, the driver of one of the buses that stopped at the hospital hooted impatiently.

Honey, left with no choice, threw her arms around his neck and once again found herself up close and very personal with Lucien Grey.

Her eyes were on a level with his mouth, her body touching every part of him from breast to knees.

His skin was warm and her fingers tangled in the wild mop of dark hair that curled over his neck. Place, pain and the presence of an irritable bus driver faded out and she found herself fighting the urge to purr.

Even as the thought sent a whisper of heat through her veins, his hands were on her waist and she was airborne.

As she held on for dear life she could feel his bones through the thin cotton of his shirt and the increase of his heartbeat as he took her weight, could hear the faint huff of effort before he dumped her unceremoniously on the passenger seat.

'That wasn't so painful, was it?' he asked.

'More painful for you than me,' she assured him, easing herself carefully round to face the front as he shut the door and climbed in beside her.

It was a long time since she'd been in such close contact with a man and now it had happened twice in two days.

She could still feel the warm skin of Lucien Grey's neck, the tickle of his hair, the hard bones of his chest as he lifted her. She was reliving the touch, the taste, of a sensuous lower lip indelibly imprinted on her memory.

And there was his sweater, a comfort as she'd lain on the deck, in the ambulance, while she'd been waiting for the X-ray, knotted around her neck. His scent, the knowledge that he'd been wearing it against his skin, lent a deeper intimacy.

Her head seemed to be spinning a little and

there was a distinct shortness of breath as long-forgotten sensations were jarred into life.

The only sensation she wasn't feeling was pain.

'How's your back?' she asked, desperate for a distraction.

'Telling me that you were right. You are no flower fairy. Can you manage the seat belt?' he asked.

She quickly fumbled for it, stabbing at the slot before he took it into his head to lean across and do it for her, finally making the connection on her third attempt.

'Done.'

He pulled down his own and, with a wave of apology to the bus driver, started the engine, pressed play on the CD player and pulled away.

The music was something classical. The clearest signal that he was done with answering her questions.

She mentally zipped her mouth and J S Bach remained uninterrupted while Lucien negotiated his way out of Maybridge.

'Why was Jenny Logan up to her neck in lambs?' she asked, once they were on the main road. 'And why was she being filmed?'

'She bought a smallholding on the border of Wales and Gloucestershire as a country bolthole a few years ago. Now she's decided to turn it into a rural skills centre and our production company is making a television series about her journey.'

'You have a production company?'

He glanced at her, clearly irritated, but said, 'We set it up a while back when she wanted to leave front line broadcasting. She had plenty of ideas but needed a partner with ready cash, a long credit line and the contacts she needed.'

'Is that what you're going to do when you've finished your book?' she asked. 'Or will you go back to front line news reporting?' Bearing in mind the obvious signs that he was suffering from PSTD, that would clearly not be a good idea.

'It's time for a change,' he said. 'Jenny's done a good job, but it's time for me to step up so that we can expand our range of programmes.'

'Is that why you were staying with her?' There had been rumours of a romance, but that had been a while ago.

He glanced at her, clearly exasperated. 'I was staying with her because my flat is let until October.'

'It sounds like the perfect set-up,' she said, 'So why are you dodging the locals in Lower Haughton when you could be down on the farm?'

'It was not the peaceful retreat I'd anticipated. In either location,' he added pointedly, and they covered the rest of the journey in silence.

'Turn down the lane,' she said once they were through the village. 'And keep going for about fifty yards. You can pull in and park in front of the stables.'

You have stables?' Lucien glanced at her with a look that suggested she was not the only one who could ask irritating questions. 'Isn't that a bit fancy for a gardener's cottage?'

'Head gardener,' she reminded him. 'But they were for the work horses used for pulling the mower in the days before the estate was mechanised, and hauling the trees felled in the wood. Now it's home to Aunt Flora's ancient car and her still room.' Catching his look, she said, 'That's where the lady of the house bottled fruit and made potions and cordials. And, in Aunt Flora's case, wine.'

'Dandelion?' he suggested as they passed a gash of vivid yellow fringing the long stone wall that fronted the cottage.

'First pick a gallon of dandelion petals...'

It was so much easier when Lucien Grey was rude, Honey decided. Stroking fantasies were blown away, along with guilt about her own sharp tongue.

'A gallon? That's an awful lot of dandelion petals.'

'It takes effort to make summer in a glass. Elderflower champagne is less work.'

She and her aunt had made that together every year when she'd been growing up. 'I was going to pick the flowers tomorrow.'

It had been such a special thing to do together until she had turned into a stroppy teenager, moaning about having to spend a precious Saturday sterilising the equipment and picking the flowers, when all she'd wanted to do was go into Maybridge and meet up with school friends.

Tomorrow had been about trying to hold on to something precious, and she blinked back the tears blurring the heavy cream blossoms in the hedgerow.

'There's always next year,' he replied. 'If you're still here. Village opinion is that there's not a lot to keep a young woman in a place like Lower Haughton.'

She fought down the lump in her throat. 'For such a recluse, Mr Grey, you seem to pick up all the gossip.'

He didn't answer as he drove through the wide gap where the gate had been leaning drunkenly open for as long as she could remember. The stable block had been built at a ninety-degree angle, sheltering the cottage from winter winds sweeping down the valley, and Lucien pulled up in the courtyard that fronted it.

'You only get a glimpse of the cottage from the towpath,' he said, looking up at the deep thatch of the roof as he walked around the vehicle, retrieved her crutches and opened the door. 'It's much bigger than I realised.'

'It was originally three cottages, but there was always someone eager to entice Jack Rose away.

Lord Hartford went to great lengths to make sure he was never tempted.'

'Jack was your great-grandfather?'

'Great-great-great-great…' She made a vague gesture, not up to counting exactly how many greats. 'He travelled all over the world on plant gathering expeditions with his lordship. His sons trained under him and all but one of them went to work for other great houses.'

'While the one left behind succeeded his father as head gardener.'

Honey nodded. 'There's always been a Rose at Orchard End.'

'And now that's you? Mrs Lacey said you inherited it, but surely it was part of the estate?'

'It was, but one of the Hartfords had a gambling habit and he sold off the estate cottages and the village properties to his tenants about fifty years ago. That way he had the cash to pay his debts, with the added bonus that he no longer had the expense of maintaining them.'

'So your great-grandfather bought it?'

'He thought it was a scandal, and refused to have anything to do with it, but Aunt Flora borrowed the money to make sure her father could stay in his home.'

'He had no sons?'

'Their names are on the village war memorial.'

'I'm sorry.'

'Yes…' They had both seen what war could

do. 'And I'm sorry if you were hoping that I had a lease that was about to expire so that you'd be rid of your annoying neighbour.'

'I'm the one with a short-term lease,' he replied, 'and your aunt made a good investment.'

'She did it for love, not profit,' Honey said, taking advantage of his distraction to slide down unaided from her seat.

The drop was further than she expected. She landed on her uninjured foot, but the jar of it went right through her body, and she was unable to stifle the squeak of pain.

Lucien turned as she reached out for something to hang onto and, before she could grab the door, he caught her, supporting her while she struggled to catch her breath.

So much for avoiding another of those heart-pounding close-ups.

'Idiot,' he said, clearly irritated by her unwillingness to rely on anyone. 'Is your key in the basket?'

'No, I've got it. If you'd just…'

He eased his hold so that she could reach her key pocket but did not let go when she had them in hand.

'Hang on,' he said as, without warning, he bent to hook his arm beneath her knees, lifting her so that she once again had to throw her hands around his neck.

'No! Stupid man! Put me down!'

He ignored her, although his knees noticeably buckled as he carried her along the path to the front door.

She fumbled to find the rarely used front door key on her key ring and slid it into the lock. As she turned it, Lucien shouldered his way in through the hall, dumping her, with every appearance of relief, on the sofa, and startling the cat, who shot behind the nearest armchair.

'Now who's the idiot?' she asked as he bent over, his hands on his knees while he recovered. 'Acting like some macho Galahad. We'd have been in a right pickle if you'd collapsed under my weight.'

Unexpectedly, Lucien began to laugh.

'What's so funny?' she demanded.

'You really do have a cat.'

'That's not how it works,' she said. 'Joseph Banks believes that this is his cottage. I'm only tolerated because I provide meaty chunks twice a day.' Then she began to laugh too. 'The cat has me. Alma and Brian took him in when Aunt Flora died,' she added, 'but he was sitting on the doorstep waiting for me on the day I arrived home.'

'Are you suggesting that he knew you were coming?'

'I'd love to think it was some feline extrasensory super power but it's more likely that he followed Alma when she came over to stock up the fridge.'

'Dogs are friendlier.'

'Is that so? Maybe you should get one,' she suggested, easing herself into a sitting position. 'For goodness' sake sit down and get your breath back.'

'I'm fine.' He straightened, hand to his back, stretching out the kinks. 'I'll make that tea. '

'That would be most welcome, but could you fetch my crutches first? I really need the bathroom.'

'Will that be upstairs or downstairs?'

'Don't even think about carrying me upstairs.'

He grimaced. 'I'm trying not to.'

'Just fetch the crutches. I can take it from there.'

The minute he was gone, Honey used the arm of the chair and her good leg to haul herself upright. She was sweating by the time he returned, but he handed her the crutches without comment and placed her basket beside the sofa.

'Don't lock the door,' he called after her as she shrugged off his sweater and swung herself in the direction of the downstairs suite that had been installed for her great-grandfather in his final years.

It had since been modernised by Flora when she had made the decision to move her bedroom downstairs. Not because she couldn't manage the stairs, she'd insisted, but to stop Honey worrying that she'd fall.

'You'll find the tea in a caddy marked "Tea",' she threw back at him, 'and the teapot in the cupboard above the kettle.'

* * *

Lucien filled the kettle and took a couple of mugs that hung from a china-laden dresser that took up half the wall of the heavily beamed kitchen. He set them on a small tray and opened the tea caddy.

A ceiling rack over the farmhouse table was hung with dried herbs, and he feared the tea would be some weird mixture created by Great-Aunt Flora. But, while the tea was loose-leaf, it had the reassuringly familiar scent of Earl Grey.

The teapot was glass with an inbuilt strainer. A teabag-in-a-mug man, he'd never made tea in a pot or used loose tea. He put in one scoop, then added another just in case. There was a bottle of milk in the fridge, and he poured some into a small matching milk jug.

The cat, a large ginger creature with a white bib and paws and impressive whiskers, had recovered from its fright and began to weave itself around his ankles, looking up and mewing pathetically.

'Sorry, Joe, feeding the cat is above my pay grade.'

'He responds, when it suits him, to Banks, and he was fed this morning. He's just trying it on.'

He turned to find his endlessly annoying neighbour watching him from the doorway. 'I didn't see any sugar.'

'I don't take it and I know you don't. There are biscuits in the tin.'

'I can't see one marked "biscuits".'

'Try the one with a botanical drawing of *rosa canina*. The dog rose,' she translated.

'Are you hungry, Miss Rose?' He'd only had a mouthful of the sandwich he'd bought since breakfast, and she'd had nothing. 'Can I get you something?'

'I don't know, Mr Grey. Can you cook?'

'I can make a sandwich. Or I could call out for something?'

'So could I, but all I want right now is a cup of tea.'

Unconvinced, he opened the biscuit tin, added some shortbread to a plate and followed her as she made her way carefully back to the sofa.

He put the tray on a low table before pulling an ancient, much-patched leather pouffe in her direction.

'It's your foot you have to keep raised, not your eyebrows,' he said, catching her look. 'Here...' He put a hand beneath her calf and lifted her foot into place. 'Have you got a bag of frozen peas for the ice pack?'

'Probably,' she said. 'Are you offering to apply it?' She didn't give him time to come up with an excuse. 'It's okay, I was just kidding, but I'll let you be Mother.'

'Milk first or second?' he asked without comment.

'Neither. I've spent too much time in parts of the world where milk is a risky option.'

'Mrs Lacey said you'd been working abroad.'

'When I should have been here. Aunt Flora insisted she was managing, had all the help she needed, but she was too old to be on her own.'

'There was no one else?'

'A couple of world wars and the Spanish flu wiped out most of the Rose family. Those that are left are far flung. Brian was doing the heavy work in the garden, and Alma did her shopping and the cleaning, but it wasn't enough.'

'It's never enough,' he said, thinking of his own mother dying of cancer while he'd been thousands of miles away reporting on the agony of strangers.

She'd hidden it from him and had kept up a cheerful front when he'd managed a moment to call. She'd been a strong, stubborn woman who didn't want to be a bother, protecting him from the worry.

And here was another one. Despite the snappy retorts, Honey was pale. 'You may not take sugar, Miss Rose, but maybe you should have a spot of honey in your tea.'

'I was bringing the last pot to you. I hope it wasn't broken.'

'No, it's safe in your basket.'

'In that case, let's both have a restorative spoonful and then you can take it home with you. And there will be more strawberries, although you'll have to come and pick them yourself,' she said as he bent to retrieve the honey from her basket. 'I don't suppose you found my missing sandal?'

He glanced at the strappy sandal she was wearing on her uninjured foot. She'd have been a lot safer sticking to the boot she'd jammed into his door.

'It will be under the deck,' he said, tearing his gaze from the elegant ankle exposed by the calf-length trousers that clung to her legs.

'Wet and muddy.' She sighed. 'If it hasn't rolled down into the river and been washed away.'

He stirred a little honey into each of the mugs. 'I'll look for it when I get back.'

'Thanks. If you give it to Alma, she'll drop it in when she's passing.' He must have looked blank because she said, 'Alma Lacey. Your housekeeper?'

'Oh, right. I didn't know that was her name.'

'You know mine.'

'Yes,' he admitted unenthusiastically. 'It's a bit of a mouthful.'

'It could have been worse. My grandmother was called Hyacinth. Can you imagine? Every time someone shouted, "Hi!" in the street, you'd turn around thinking it was you.'

'You can take the horticultural theme too far,' he agreed.

'It's family tradition. Every girl born into the Rose family is given the name of a flower or shrub doing its thing that month.'

'They're all there.' She made a vague gesture at a stand on which rested a large family bible. 'I'm the last entry.'

'Honeysuckle.'

Her smile was worth the effort. 'Bravo, Mr Grey.'

'Rose suits you better.'

'Because of the thorns, no doubt.' Large blue eyes glinted back at him with a look he couldn't quite decipher. A look tugging at an elusive memory...

'If we're sticking with horticulture, surely "Nettle" would be more appropriate?' he suggested.

For a moment he thought he'd gone too far, but after a pause, when it might have gone either way, she laughed.

'You have to be the rudest man I've ever met. But if you'll drop the "miss", I can live with Rose.'

'Which means that I lose any right to object if you choose to call me Grey.'

The smile widened. 'That's the way the cookie crumbles, Mr Grey. You have to make your decision and live with it.'

CHAPTER FIVE

'Life is like a rose garden—watch for the thorns and keep the pest spray handy.'
—Anonymous

LUCIEN GRITTED HIS TEETH.

Thorns…

Honeysuckle Rose had been a thorn in his flesh since the moment he'd made the mistake of answering her furious hammering on his front door. And yet, despite the nettles, her quick tongue and the hours wasted at the hospital, it was the taste of strawberries that he couldn't shake off.

Had he kissed her? The memory seemed more real every time he thought about it and yet it seemed unlikely. She wasn't a woman to hold back…

He picked up a mug and offered it to her.

'Your tea, Honey.'

He'd anticipated a smile, amusement or triumph. But, instead of taking the mug, she placed her hand around his. 'It's a bit hot for the moment, but thank you, Lucien. For the tea. And for everything you did today.'

Her touch was gentle, disturbingly intimate, and for a moment he was in danger of spilling hot tea over her hand and her sofa.

'What was I going to do? Leave you with your leg stuck in a hole?'

Now she smiled. 'Are you saying that you weren't tempted? Not even for a moment?'

'I'll plead the fifth on that one,' he said, returning the mug to the tray. 'Do you need your painkillers?'

She glanced at a tall casement clock in the corner. 'Not for another hour.'

'In that case, why don't you lie down for a while?'

Wonder of wonders she didn't argue when he pulled down a large soft cushion and propped it against the arm of the sofa for her to lie back against. Didn't object when he lifted both her legs so that she could turn around and stretch out.

There was nothing but a barely discernible shiver, but the walls of the cottage were thick and, despite the fact that it was a warm day, it was cool inside.

'Are you cold?' he asked.

'Just a bit. There's an Afghan on the armchair.'

Banks had taken up residence and hissed his disapproval at being disturbed. Lucien gave him back a hard stare, jerked the colourful knitted blanket from under him and spread it over Honey's long legs.

He took her painkillers from her basket, programmed his number into her phone and then placed everything within easy reach on the table.

'Call me if you need anything.'

She responded with a wry smile, no doubt hearing the difference between the invitation and the hope that she would do no such thing.

'I've taken up enough of your time, Lucien. I won't keep you from your book.'

'It's not going anywhere.' In every meaning of the word.

'It must be difficult,' she said. 'Having to relive what you've seen.'

He lifted his shoulders, shrugging it off, because what could he say?

'Did you keep a diary?' she asked.

'An audio diary...' Listening to it, hearing the background soundtrack of explosions, crying children and men and women wailing in grief, was tearing lumps out of him. 'When you're constantly on the move, notebooks get lost. It's safer to download it to the cloud every night.'

'Our smart phones...what would we do without them.' It was a statement rather than a question and didn't require a response. 'It's important. What you're doing.'

'Is it? I sometimes wonder.' For a moment their eyes locked and there was a repeat of that *déjà vu* moment, the feeling that it had happened before.

'You've done more than enough, Lucien.'

He should have seized on her dismissal with relief, gratitude, at being released from any further obligation. Instead, he found himself wishing that he'd been less abrasive. Was welcome in this peaceful room instead of someone she clearly wished she'd never set eyes on.

'Are you ready to risk the tea now?' he asked.

'Please.' He placed the mug in her hands and she wrapped her fingers around it, welcoming the warmth, taking a sip and sighing with pleasure. 'You really don't have to stay, you know. I'll be fine.'

'I was rather hoping to finish my tea before you kicked me out. And have a piece of what looks like home-made shortbread,' he said when common sense, and every other kind of sense, was urging him to grab the chance to escape.

'Help yourself,' she said. 'But do sit down. I'm getting a crick in my neck looking up at you.'

He took a piece of the shortbread and bit into it as he crossed to the armchair vacated by Banks, who'd followed the Afghan to the sofa and settled in the corner near Honey's feet.

The soft leather was aged with wear, and as he sank into it it wrapped around him like a hug. It felt familiar, like coming home—something he hadn't experienced in a very long time.

'This is very good,' he said, distracting himself from the thought with the shortbread. 'Did you make it?'

'Aunt Flora used to bake it for Brian to have with his tea when he was working in the garden. Making it helps to keep her spirit alive.'

'Like the elderflower champagne?'

She pulled a face. 'It's stupid, I know. She's gone…' she murmured, doing her best to brush off what was clearly a painful loss.

'It's what we do when we lose someone,' he said. 'A way of keeping them with us. My mother loved custard creams. I can't stand them, but I always seem to have a packet around somewhere.'

'How long since you lost her?'

'Five years. Cancer. My father took off when I was a baby,' he added without thinking. It was a rejection that he never talked about. Not even Jenny knew…

'That must have been tough for both of you.'

'It's a common enough story. What about your parents?' he asked in an effort to deflect any more questions. 'Are they close enough to come and take care of you?'

'They died in a road accident more than twenty years ago. I've lived here ever since.'

'I'm so sorry to hear that. It was good of your aunt to take you in. It feels like a refuge,' he said. 'This room…'

Oak beams, a deep inglenook fireplace, and rich dark green velvet curtains that in winter would shut out the draughts.

He could see the rear garden through a pair of French windows that opened onto a terrace and beyond it the meadow lawn. From this distance the blossom in the orchard looked like an Impressionist painting and the only sound was the ticking of the casement clock.

Realising that Honey was watching him, waiting, he said, 'It would be easy to believe that I've slipped back a century.'

'It's the beams. Aunt Flora used to say that oak doesn't know it's dead, that it continues to breathe.'

'Your Aunt Flora sounds...'

'A bit potty?' she suggested, when he hesitated. 'I know, it's mad, but close your eyes and listen. Breathe with it.'

Aware that he was putting off the moment when he had to return to his desk and a world filled with pain, he closed his eyes.

In her fury, Honey had missed the chance to introduce herself and remind Lucien that they had met before, and now it was too late. Against all inclination he'd been kind today, and she had no wish to embarrass him with the news that he'd failed to recognise the nurse who'd cleaned his wound and stitched him up in the chaos of a refugee camp.

In that heightened atmosphere, with the sound of fighting getting nearer, that heart-jolting connection had felt important, but it had been no more than a fleeting moment. It would barely have registered in Lucien Grey's hectic life. That it had stayed with her only demonstrated the emptiness in hers.

She watched as the tension left his shoulders, his breathing changed, and he slipped into what she could see was much-needed sleep.

It was a kind of magic.

It was how her aunt had soothed her, helped her to sleep, when she had first come to Orchard End, too young to understand the finality of death. All she'd wanted was for her mother to come back and give her a hug, for her father to swing her up into the air.

She'd learned to use the technique herself when stressed about exams and her brain wouldn't stop whirling.

And during that awful time when, six days after Nicholas had put his ring on her finger, promising to be back to marry her in six months, she'd heard about his death on the ten o'clock news and her world had collapsed for the second time.

And after Flora's death when her body—held together for so long by little more than sheer will-power—was no longer able to keep up the lie that everything was all right and Honey had become a medical evacuee.

Sleep…'nature's sweet restorer'…was a gift that she gladly gave Lucien Grey. Gratefully accepted as she closed her own eyes and listened to the ancient oak breathe.

When Lucien opened his eyes, it took a moment for the room, the garden and the ticking clock to come into focus and for him to realise where he was. A moment for it all to come rushing back.

How long had he been asleep? The mug beside him was cold. He looked at the sofa, certain that Honey would be watching him, amused, but she too had fallen asleep.

The only watcher was the cat, who blinked lazily, yawned and stretched. He held his breath as it stood up, turned around, then settled back down, but Honey didn't stir.

The temptation was to close his own eyes and sink back into the rare oblivion of a dreamless sleep. Instead, he forced himself to his feet and very quietly carried everything out to the kitchen, put the milk away in the fridge and rinsed the mugs and plates, leaving them to drain.

He filled a glass with water and placed it on the table beside the painkillers, hesitating for a moment, uncertain whether he should wake her. And found himself looking down into her open eyes.

'Is there anything you need before I leave?' he asked.

'No…' There was a hesitation, as if she had thought of something but it was too much effort to summon it up.

'I haven't forgotten your shoe,' he assured her, but her lids were drooping and, even before he'd finished speaking, she was asleep again. He doubted that she'd been truly awake.

He closed the front door as quietly as he could,

checking that it was locked. Then stood for a moment, gathering himself.

His neighbour was an unsettling mix of sweet and sharp and he'd been off-balance ever since he'd opened his front door yesterday. She'd left, but her presence had remained, prickling over him like the faint burn of the nettles that still tingled beneath the skin.

As he stepped out of the shelter of the porch, he was assailed by the scent of the rose scrambling over the thatch. It was covered with a mass of fat little buds, but a few small, semi-double flowers had opened in the warm May sunshine, and they showered him with pale pink petals as he brushed passed.

With his arms full of woman, he'd barely noticed the garden. Now he could see that it was crammed with spring colour. Not just the conventional flowers, but familiar tall pink spikes of something he only knew as fire weed, the first plant to colonise bomb sites. And the frothy white stuff that grew along the hedgerows. Both were weeds, but the bees and butterflies clearly appreciated them.

And scrambling through the trees were the flowers that were on the biscuit tin. *Rosa canina*. And honeysuckle. So, May was her birthday month. Wasn't that a flower too?

Not that it mattered. He wasn't about to send

her a bunch of roses—or honeysuckle, come to that.

Nettles, now. He could definitely be tempted…

He ducked as a swallow nearly scalped him before disappearing under the cottage eaves. Orchard End was teeming with life, with renewal, and his own senses seemed sharper, more aware, as he breathed in the scent.

It was easy to see why Honey thought his own garden was sterile. Why she'd been so angry that he'd put hers at risk. A dower house, he knew, was a place for a widow to move into when her son married and her daughter-in-law took her title, her place. A home for a woman who had all the time in the world to lavish on her garden.

Until now, he hadn't noticed anything wrong. Hadn't noticed anything much if he was honest with himself. He was noticing now as he walked down to the boat house in search of Honey's missing shoe.

When you took the trouble to look, it was easy to spot the slightly darker green shapes where flower beds had been cleared, flattened and reseeded in order to reduce the maintenance costs.

No pruning, no weeding, just an unobstructed lawn to be kept in check with a ride-on mower. But where was the colour, the scent, the movement of insects? He understood the practicalities, but the reality was depressing. Even weeds, he thought, had to be better than this.

He reached the boat house and looked round. Honey was right. It was in a dangerous condition, which was perhaps why no one had mentioned it. He'd contact the agent and warn Mrs Lacey to stay clear. He didn't want any more accidents.

He took rather more care crossing the decking and groped under the deck until he found Honey's shoe. It was, as she'd feared, wet and muddy but, once he'd cleaned it, he'd leave it for Mrs Lacey...

Which was when he let slip an expletive.

Honey was half asleep when the phone rang. She reached for it, planning to switch it off, then blinked as she saw the caller's name.

'Lucien...?'

'Honey. How are you?'

'I've just woken up. Is there a problem?'

'Well, the good news is that I have your shoe.'

'The bad news, I take it, is that it's ruined.'

'No. I've cleaned it up and it'll be fine once it's dry.'

'Great. So what's the bad news?'

'You said that I'd done enough, which suggests you had someone else in mind to call if you needed anything. If it was Mrs Lacey, I have to tell you that she's on the other side of the county, baking for a party before heading for sand and sangria in Spain. She's going to be away for the next two weeks.'

'The party is this weekend? Brian mentioned it

when he came round last week with some plants. Brian's her husband,' she explained. 'He must have told me when they were away, but I couldn't have been paying attention. But it's not a problem.'

'No, it isn't. I'll bring the sandal round myself.'

'There's no need. Honestly. I won't be wearing it for the next couple of weeks.'

'I know, but you did mention calling out for something to eat.'

'Did I?' She frowned. 'I don't believe I actually said that. Only that I was capable of it. I'll probably just scramble some eggs.'

'I imagine you could do that by looking at them,' he assured her.

'That would be a useful skill, but sadly I need heat and a saucepan like everyone else.'

'You're going to have to work on your spells.'

'Are you suggesting that I'm a witch, Lucien?'

'There's definitely something a little bit...'

'A little bit what?'

'It'll come to me,' he said. 'But forget the eggs. I have a very generous lasagne left by Mrs Lacey. Far more than I'll be able to manage.'

Was he offering to share?

'It would be a pity to waste it,' he prompted, when Honey, for once lost for words, said nothing. 'I'll bring it when I drop off your shoe.'

Her stomach rumbled. She hadn't eaten anything since breakfast and Alma's cooking was always a treat.

'You could make it last for two days,' she pointed out.

Because it was a fact.

And she was an idiot.

'I could,' he acknowledged, 'but she's filled the freezer and there's a curry with tomorrow's date on it. I'd hate to mess up her system.'

Lucien Grey didn't have the look of a man who would be dictated to by a date written on a freezer pack, but her ankle was swollen inside the boot and her foot was throbbing painfully. The thought of standing while she made even the simplest of suppers was not appealing.

'Would that be one of Alma's legendary chicken curries?' she asked.

'Can I hear you drooling?'

Having given him every opportunity to get out of his guilty obligation to be a good neighbour, Honey finally conceded to hunger. 'Possibly.'

'Then you know that you would be doing me an enormous favour by saving me from tomorrow's leftovers,' he said, seriously heavy on the sarcasm.

'A big enough favour for a share of the curry?' Afraid she might have pushed him too far— that lasagne was calling her name—she quickly added, 'Just kidding. Did you lock the front door when you left?'

'I did,' he assured her.

'Not a problem. Only strangers come to the front in the country, and it'll be quicker if you come along the towpath. You'll find the back door key under a stone frog.' Then, as an afterthought, 'You could pop into the glasshouse as you pass and pick some salad leaves.'

'I have never "popped" anywhere in my life,'

'Hop, step, jump…' she suggested, at which point she discovered that she was talking to herself.

'That was bad, Banks.' The cat blinked at her. 'No, really. He feels guilty about the butterflies,' she continued as she rubbed behind his ear. 'Which he should. But, while he's wishing me to the devil, and I suspect a gnat's whisker from calling me a witch, it seems that he's determined to do his duty as a good neighbour. So I really ought to stop…'

Stop what?

Stop pricking him, teasing him? Smile and say thank you nicely…? Too late for that. He would think she was faking it even if she wasn't.

She'd fled the kindness of people when she'd arrived home too late to hold Flora's hand as she slipped away, staying only long enough to bury her and make arrangements with Alma and Brian to look after the cottage and take care of Banks. That done, she'd rushed back to the refugee camp where she could hide her self-pitying tears in the misery around her. Bury her guilt in helping strangers.

And it had worked until the moment she'd hit

an emotional wall and the ground had come up to meet her. She'd been home a couple of months but, while she hadn't removed her door knocker like Lucien, she had found excuses to turn down invitations to village coffee mornings and to join the book club or the village fete committee. She'd shielded herself from what she felt to be the undeserved sympathy of people who had known her most of her life.

Unlike Lucien, however, who had a tenant in his flat and a film crew at the retreat offered by Jenny Logan, she'd returned to the healing peace of her childhood home, the welcome of the bees and a garden that needed her. Even a cat who grudgingly offered a pretence at affection in return for food and a favourite chair.

Lucien Grey might be an antisocial grouch, but she knew enough of what he'd seen and been through to have been kinder.

'Bugger…' she muttered, grabbing her crutches and heading for the bathroom. 'Must try harder.'

CHAPTER SIX

*'Remember me when I am gone away,
Gone far away into the silent land;
When you can no more hold me by the hand,
Nor I half turn to go yet turning stay.'*
—Christina Rossetti

HONEY PULLED A face at her reflection. The make-up she'd applied before leaving the cottage that morning had been minimal, and now it was history. Despite the long doze on the sofa, there were dark smudges under her eyes, and the surgical collar had to be the least flattering accessory known to man.

Lipstick might help, but the only one to hand was bright red, which would make her look like a clown.

As if it mattered.

Lucien Grey would neither notice nor care what she looked like. He'd leave the shoe, the lasagne, and possibly some salad leaves if she was lucky, before retreating to the safety of the Dower House.

The fact that she had even thought about wearing it made her put it down. She simply washed her face, brushed her hair and tied it back with a clip, then raided her aunt's wardrobe for a clean long-sleeved black top that hung down to her hips.

* * *

Damn the woman!

Lucien cut the connection before he said something he'd regret.

Not that it would bother her. She'd come right back with some smart reply. Honeysuckle Rose... The most inappropriate name ever.

In a moment of weakness, he'd offered to share his supper, and in return she'd teased him, laughed at him and given him orders...

When he'd spotted her heading towards the boat house he should have turned round and gone back to the peace and quiet of his study.

Except that it wasn't quiet, not in his head. And there was no peace. At least when he was trading insults with her he could forget about the horrors in his head for a few minutes.

Annoying as she was, he found himself saying stuff to her that he'd never told anyone. Normally that would have had him running for the hills, but it was refreshing to be with someone who wasn't walking around him as if treading on eggshells...

He picked up the lasagne, collected the damp shoe from the porch and headed down the garden towards the towpath.

He'd always been running down here before, driving himself to move, not seeing anything but the empty space in front of him and hearing only the thud of his feet and the occasional irritable quack and flutter of wings as a duck flapped out of his way.

He set off briskly enough—he couldn't run with the dish in his hand—until frantic cheeping caught his attention. He slowed, looked round and saw a flotilla of newly hatched ducklings, tiny balls of fluff, scurrying through the water to keep up with their mother.

He watched until they disappeared beneath the overhanging branches of a willow and, pushing open the back gate of Orchard End, he realised that for the first time in months he was smiling.

Not forcing it in order to be polite, or because people were being kind, but without having to think about it.

The large stone frog by the back door doubled as a flowerpot, and as he lifted it to retrieve the key it released the pungent, pine-like scent of rosemary.

It was likely that the whole village knew where the key was kept, but he'd learned a little about country living while staying at Jenny's and, having unlocked the door, he returned it to its hiding place.

'Hello?'

Getting no answer, he left the shoe on the rack in the mud room and uncovered the lasagne and slid it into the hottest part of the Aga before glancing into the living room. It was empty, so he returned to the garden in search of the glasshouse.

Long, with a sloping roof and clearly very old, it had been built against the rear of the stables. It was filled with small plants in seed trays, larger plants in pots and plants growing in a border against the wall. And there were salad leaves on the bench.

By the time Honey made it through to the kitchen, Lucien was rinsing the leaves he'd picked under the cold tap.

'I've left your shoe in the mud room and I've put the lasagne in the oven,' he said.

'As long as it's not the other way around.'

'I don't know. The shoe would keep your foot company in your mouth,' he said, finally turning round, eyebrow raised, inviting an answer.

'It's certainly big enough,' she admitted, remembering her determination to be kinder.

His gaze dropped to her mouth.

He had eyes the colour of bitter chocolate, emphasised by a fan of pale lines where they had been screwed up against sun too bright for sunglasses to offer total protection. A mop of dark curls that hadn't seen a barber in months and a close-cropped beard that was little more than stubble. Pretty much the way he'd looked the day he had stumbled into the medical centre with his arm in a mess. Only the dust was missing.

Now, with dark shadows not only around but in his eyes, the image was dramatically heightened.

It was all Honey could do to stop herself from putting her arms around him, doing whatever it took to ease the pain she saw in his face. Or maybe it was her own pain she hoped to forget, if only briefly. Maybe if he'd remembered her...

As if reading her thoughts, he turned abruptly and began opening drawers until he found mats and cutlery.

She watched for a moment until she realised that he was laying two places. 'You're staying?'

'It seemed more eco-friendly to use one oven.' He looked up. 'I thought you'd appreciate that.'

'I... Yes...'

'Go on, say it. You know you want to.'

She started, dragged back from the thought of how his skin would feel beneath her fingers, the way his stomach would tighten in anticipation beneath her palm...

'Wh-what?'

'That if I'm staying, I'll have to wash up.'

'Heaven forbid!' she exclaimed, relieved that he couldn't actually read her mind. Then, in case he thought she was going soft, because, like smiling and saying thank you nicely, he'd think anything else was fake, 'Just load the dishwasher before you go.'

He shook his head. 'Tell me, Honey. How have you lived so long?'

'It's a mystery,' she admitted, conscious of him watching her as she eased her way across to one of the cupboards, keeping the maximum distance between them.

'What are you doing?'

'I'm going to make a salad dressing.'

'You're lucky to have it. The salad. The plants were flagging in the heat of the glasshouse.'

'Oh…sugar! I watered when I opened up this morning, but it has been very warm today. I'll go out later—'

'No need. I've sprayed the trays, watered the salad pots and left the hose running on the bed to give them a soak. I think everything will survive.'

'Lucien…'

'I've never had a garden, but I do know that plants need water.'

'Never?'

'There's nowhere to dig in an inner-city tower block. Did you manage to rescue the caterpillars?' he asked, abruptly changing the subject.

'Well, I rehomed them on the towpath nettles. And the red admirals are in an old aquarium in the mud room. Some of them might survive.'

'I'm glad to hear it.' Then, 'Have you forgotten that you're supposed to keep your foot up as much as possible?'

'No, but…'

'That would be the "but" that negates everything that goes before it?' he asked.

'I hoped you might have forgotten that.'

Forgotten the words, remembered her…

'Why? You meant every word.'

She gave an awkward little shrug and would have nodded but for the collar. Hating the restriction, she ripped it off and flung it away.

'Should you have done that?'

'Probably not,' she admitted. 'But it was annoying me.'

'And we both know how that goes,' he said, pulling out a chair for her. 'In your own time.'

'This feels all wrong,' she said, sitting down.

'Because you're the one usually taking care of people?'

She held her breath. He had remembered…

'You told the paramedic that you're a nurse,' he said, pulling out a second chair for her foot. 'Have you done the ice pack thing?'

'Not yet,' she said, swallowing down her disappointment. 'I'll do it after supper.'

'It's true, then. Doctors and nurses really do make the worst patients.'

'No. I'll do it after supper and then go to bed. Right now, I need to make the salad dressing, which I can do perfectly well sitting down.'

'And how will you do that?'

'By asking you to pass me the ingredients,' she said. And smiled with all the insincerity she could muster, because that was what he'd expect.

He shook his head. 'Tell me what you need.'

'Olive oil, Dijon mustard, white wine vinegar, salt… Top left-hand corner cupboard.'

'Bowl?' he prompted when he'd found everything.

'In the dresser. And a small jug.' When he'd found them, she pointed up at the rack hanging over the table from which hung not only dried plants but kitchen gadgets. 'And that whisk.'

'What would you like to drink, with the lasagne?'

'A glass of something dark red and Italian but, since I'm on painkillers and antibiotics, I'll stick to water.'

'Was it very bad?' he asked. 'The injury?'

'Was it very bad? Let me think,' she said, finger to cheek in mock deliberation. 'Filthy wood rammed into my heel, massive infection risk, antitetanus jab, grade two sprain...' She paused as he muttered an expletive. 'Quite,' she agreed. 'But on the plus side I only partially tore a ligament and didn't break any bones. It could have been a lot worse.'

'It sounds horrendous. How long will you be on crutches?'

'As long as it takes.' About to tell him to help himself to wine or beer, it occurred to her that, if he was suffering from PTSD, he shouldn't have alcohol or caffeine.

He checked in the fridge, then looked at her. 'Where will I find the water?'

'In the tap?'

She was concentrating on the dressing when

he knelt beside her and set about pulling free the Velcro strips holding the boot on her foot.

'What are you doing!'

'Applying an ice pack.' He stopped as he saw the compression bandage. 'Your toes are bruised…'

'That will happen.'

'I'm surprised you didn't scream the place down.'

'I was in enough trouble…' She gasped and grabbed his arm as he placed something ice-cold over her ankle.

'Did that hurt?'

'Do you care?' His face was level with hers and she saw the muscle tighten in his jaw. 'I'm sorry. I didn't mean that…'

'It's okay,' he said. 'I recognise a defence mechanism when I hear it.'

'I'm not—'

'It's why I left the farm and rented the Dower House,' he said, cutting off her denial. 'There came a point when Jenny, realising that if I had to force one more smile my face would crack in half, took pity on me and found this place.'

'You don't have to smile at me.'

'No…' He looked up and met her gaze head on. 'You are without doubt the neighbour from hell, but I don't have to pretend with you.'

'You're welcome.'

And there it was. A smile. Not one of those big, all-singing, all-dancing smiles that was all for show. It was no more than a shift of muscles. The deepening of a crease carved into his cheek at the corner of his eyes. Hardly noticeable at all unless you were conscious of every movement.

Realising that she was still clutching his arm, she let go, but as she'd reached out to grab him her cuff had ridden up and now he was staring at her wrist.

'Would you turn off the hose before the glass-house floods, Lucien?' she asked, self-consciously tugging her sleeve down.

'What…? Oh, yes.'

'And close it up while you're out there?'

He nodded and, when he had gone, Honey sat for a moment, her hand wrapped tightly round her wrist covering the narrow circle of forget-me-nots that was usually hidden by the wide strap of her smart watch.

She'd removed it at some point in the hospital and forgotten it.

Lucien paused at the kitchen door to gather his thoughts. Honey had a tattoo?

That wasn't unusual, but he knew he'd seen it before somewhere. So it followed that he must have seen her. The odd moments he'd been experiencing ever since she'd appeared on his doorstep were not his subconscious playing tricks with his mind. They were real memories.

But why hadn't he recognised her? And why hadn't she said anything?

While he'd never heard her name before—who would ever forget it?—they had somehow been close enough for him to have got a close look at her wrist. Had they shaken hands at some event? Most women would have said something. Reminded him that they'd met before.

But Honey wasn't most women. Maybe when he hadn't immediately recognised her she'd let it go rather than make him feel awkward…

The thought made him smile. As if. This was a woman who never thought before she spoke.

He rubbed at the scar on his arm, still itching from the nettle sting, and in that instant it all came rushing back. The reason her eyes had sparked a flashback, the remembered pain sending him reeling back from the doorstep…

He'd been told that the woman who'd inherited the cottage had been working abroad but he hadn't cared enough to ask where, or what she was doing.

Even when she'd told the paramedics that she was a nurse he hadn't made the connection that the woman with the English country garden name had been there, in the middle of the horror when a refugee camp had become the front line and he'd become one of the casualties.

Honeysuckle Rose was the nurse who'd cleaned and stitched his wound while he'd continued talking into the camera, sending in a report of the bombing.

She'd been anonymous in scrubs, her hair covered, most of her face hidden by a surgical mask, and he'd been on his feet even while she'd been trotting out the standard warnings about the danger of infection, septicaemia. Telling him that he needed to be medevacked for further treatment and plastic surgery, all the while knowing that he'd do nothing of the kind.

She'd pulled off the gloves she'd been wearing with a snap, binning them and reaching for a fresh pair ready for the next patient when, remembering his manners, he'd turned to thank her. That was when he'd seen the circle of small flowers tattooed around her wrist like a memory bracelet. One worn by someone who in her everyday life couldn't wear jewellery.

It had been a jolt, a reminder that this was about the injured crowded outside waiting for help but with none of his privileges. Angry at the horror around him, instead of thanking her he'd been going to ask if she'd be giving the rest of the injured the same advice and had found himself looking into a pair of dark blue eyes flashing back at him, her anger equal to his own.

She'd understood…had felt the same outrage…

At that moment he'd found himself looking at a different story but, before he'd been able to speak, a shell had landed close enough to shake the makeshift medical centre. His cameraman had caught the moment when the air had filled with dust and screams. That film, with him filthy and bandaged as he'd described the scene, had led the news bulletin that night, and later that year had won them both an award.

But after that he'd been unable to keep the distance between him and the story. And now she was here. Living next door to him. It felt like fate…

He turned off the hose, closed the windows, shut the door and returned to the kitchen.

'All done,' he said.

'Thanks. That was above and beyond.'

'Hardly. Honey—'

'From the smell coming from the oven, I think the lasagne is done. If you could get rid of the ice pack before I freeze to death?'

He removed the pack of peas, then knelt beside her to refasten the boot.

'Why didn't you mention that we'd crossed paths before?' he asked, concentrating on tightening the straps.

'When would I have done that?' she asked. 'While I was having a go at you over the nettles?' She managed a wry smile. 'I think I said more than enough. For which I apologised in my note.'

'I wrote a note too. Apologising for anything I might have done. I have moments when things get away from me…' He looked up then, waiting for her to tell him exactly what he'd done in that moment when things had slipped out of kilter.

'Why don't we just draw a line under yesterday,' she suggested, 'and enjoy our supper?'

No. There could be only one reason why his lips had tasted of strawberries…

'It's hazy, but afterwards my lips tasted of strawberries. I kissed you…'

'Heightened emotions,' she said. 'Anger. We were carried away by the moment. I understood what happened to you, Lucien.' She gave an awkward little shrug. 'I had no such excuse.'

'You didn't say anything.'

'I thought it was something you'd rather not be reminded of.'

'I'm an idiot, but not that much of an idiot. It's your eyes,' he said, unable to let it go. 'I knew there was something. It was there, just on the edge of my memory.'

'I was masked up. And you were too busy talking into the camera while I cleaned you up to notice me.'

'I did more than notice you.'

He stood up abruptly, walked across to the stove, moved the lasagne to the table, filled a couple of glasses with water, then sat down opposite her.

'I came back to look for you when things had calmed down, but you'd been evacuated.'

She frowned. 'Why would you do that?'

'Because when I asked if anyone else would be medevacked out of there, your anger singed me. And I got it, Honey. You thought I was some entitled jerk who was wasting your time when there were women, children, whole families, with no means of escape.'

'No. You were doing an important job, but you were angry too.'

'At that moment I was angry with the world.'

They exchanged a look that acknowledged their mutual horror of the situation in which they'd found themselves.

'We did what we could with what we had,' she said.

'I know.' He cut into the pasta, dividing it between two plates. 'I was going to ask if I could shadow you for a while, so that I could show the world what you were doing. I believed it was a story that people at home should see.'

'You didn't need me for that, Lucien. There are people in refugee camps all over the world doing the same thing every day of their lives. Any one of them would have given you your story.'

'Maybe.' He offered her a plate, but did not let go when she took it, forcing her to look up and meet his gaze. 'But with you it was personal.'

'That's ridiculous. We scarcely exchanged a word. You didn't even know my name.'

'Sometimes,' he said, 'a look is all it takes.'

CHAPTER SEVEN

*Honeysuckle, covered in clusters of scented
tubular flowers from late spring, signifies
happiness, devotion and everlasting bonds.*

HONEY DIDN'T DENY IT. She had never forgotten that
moment, the look they'd exchanged. The realisa-
tion that his anger at the futility of war matched
her own. For a moment if had felt as if she'd found
a kindred spirit.

And yesterday there had been another of those
looks as they'd faced one another down on his
doorstep. A look that, for a moment, had sent
him spinning back into a very dark place, ending with a kiss that had left them both confused
and shaken.

She knew that place, had woken screaming
from dreams in which she couldn't hold onto people who were slipping from her grasp, overcome
with loss. If her expression had been as raw with
need as his, that crazy doorstep kiss had been inevitable.

She shook off the darkness.

'When will the book be finished?' she asked,
as she dressed the salad.

He raised an eyebrow at her abrupt change of
subject, but let it go.

'The publisher is set to release it in the autumn. The cover is done, blurbs written, but I've gone stale on it. It feels like the same old book that every front line journalist has ever written.'

'Looking in from the outside? Detached? Keeping their distance?'

'It has to be that way. You're there to record the story, not become part of it,' he said.

'So, what happened at Bouba al-Asad?' she asked.

'I mislaid my detachment in a field hospital when I came face to face with a nurse who shared my anger.'

'I'm sorry.'

'I'm not. But what I did that day was unprofessional. The building could have come down at any time. I had no one to miss me, but I put my cameraman in danger, and his wife did not hold back when I met her at the awards later that year.'

'That wasn't anger, Lucien, that was fear.'

'And she was right to be afraid. I thought she was going to hit me with that damn trophy.'

Honey frowned. 'Surely he was well clear, filming you as you dug that family out of the rubble?'

He shook his head. 'Dave gave up yelling at me to stay back and got stuck in beside me. Some of it was filmed on a mobile phone by a kid who sold it to the networks.'

She reached across the table and turned over one of his hands, stroking her fingers over the dark lines where concrete dust had become embedded.

'When I was training,' she said, 'there was an old man on the ward who'd been a miner. He'd been caught in a tunnel collapse as a young man and had marks very like these on his back.'

For a moment he let his hand lie there, warm against her palm, then shook his head.

'I lost my head for a moment,' he said, retrieving his hand to pick up his fork. 'You were the human dimension in that conflict, Honey. Hands on, helping every day. Your story is the one that people should read, not mine. How long were you working for the aid agency?'

She didn't answer and he looked up, assuming that she had a mouthful of food, but her grip on the fork had tightened.

'My first tour was in West Africa…' She swallowed. 'It was just over six years ago.'

He frowned. 'The Ebola crisis?' She nodded and he let slip an expletive. No wonder she didn't want to talk about it. 'That was a tough posting.'

'I was needed.'

'I can't begin to imagine how bad it must have been.'

For a moment all she could manage was a nod while she caught her breath and took a sip of water.

'I'm sorry. You don't have to talk about it.'

'The worst of the major outbreak was over by

the time I got there,' she said. 'Since then, it's been refugee camps. What about you?' she asked, turning the conversation back to him.

It was obvious that she didn't want to talk about her involvement in disaster response, and he didn't want to talk about the things he'd seen. So gradually, between mouthfuls, they shared details about a few days grabbed on a beach in Turkey, his visit to Petra and hers to the Valley of the Kings.

Similar interests, similar pleasures…

'And now you're home in the peace of Lower Haughton, taking care of the weeds,' he said.

Honey startled herself with a laugh. The evening had passed in what felt like a flash. It had been an age since she'd talked to someone—really talked…

'A weed,' she informed him, 'is only a flower growing in the wrong place, and even those need help. It's not that easy to grow a wildflower meadow. Grass is a bit of a thug. Its roots have to be kept in check if anything but daisies and dandelions are to grow.'

'I know nothing about gardening,' he admitted, 'but when I walked down to the boat house to find your shoe I could see where there had once been flower beds.'

'What they did there was nothing short of vandalism.' She shook her head. 'There's fruit, or some ice-cream in the freezer, if you'd like some?'

'No, I'm done. I could make some coffee, if I haven't outstayed my welcome?'

'It's a little late.'

'Of course,' he said, getting to his feet. 'You've had a stressful day. I'll clear up and leave you in peace.'

'It's a little late for coffee,' she said. 'And I'm sure you've been advised to cut down on caffeine. But, since you're offering, I'll take a camomile tea. You should try it. It's relaxing and aids sleep.'

'Do I have to go out and pick it?' he asked.

Oh, the temptation...

She gave herself a mental slap on the wrist and said, 'Not this time. You'll find a box of bags in the cupboard above the kettle, and I vote we take it outside. Now the sun's gone down, we might be lucky enough to see some bats.'

'Bats?'

'Pipistrelles. Don't worry, they're small, and they'll be more interested in feeding on insects than building a nest in your hair.'

'Are you suggesting that I need a haircut?' The light caught on the glint of silver as he raked his fingers through the mass of dark curls.

'Not for me,' she said, then blushed a little. 'Or the bats.'

'Most women I've met are scared witless by them,' he said. 'But then you are an original.'

'Thank you.'

'I'm glad you took it as a compliment.'

'A woman whose next birthday begins with

three, and dresses early nineteen-forties allotment, has to take them wherever she finds them.'

Lucien looked as if he was going to say more but clearly thought better of it. Having put on the kettle, he cleared the table and stacked everything in the dishwasher. He might be tactless, if not downright rude, but he hadn't had to bring her supper or clear up afterwards. And he had watered her drooping plants.

You could forgive a man who saw a need and, unasked, stepped in to fill it pretty much anything.

Ten minutes later they were sitting outside on a bench beneath a honeysuckle-draped pergola, mugs in hand.

'I missed this so much when I was overseas,' Honey said. 'The long, soft English dusk. The small sounds of birds settling.' And to tease him a little. 'The scent of honeysuckle.'

He closed his eyes and leaned back. 'If I'd had this, I don't think I'd have ever left.' He glanced across at her. 'You obviously love it here, so why did you leave?'

'My mother was a nurse. I have a picture of her in her uniform.' She looked at him. 'I barely remembered her, Lucien, and I thought if I could do what she did it would bring her closer.'

'Did it?'

'I don't know. I did the things she did, took my nursing degree at the same place she did. I fell in love at the same age she met my father. But I'll never know how she felt about anything.'

'You told the paramedic that you trained in London.'

'At King's. It offered a chance to work in Africa and east Asia but I don't know if that's why my mother chose it. There are so many things I'll never know.'

He understood that loss. Who was his father? Where was he now? There were so many gaps...

'You always wanted to travel?' he asked.

She shrugged. 'I'm a Rose. It's in the genes. What did you leave behind, Lucien?'

'Concrete, diesel fumes... No honeysuckle.' He turned to look at her. 'Why didn't your family call you May? After the blossom,' he added, when she raised her eyebrows at the abrupt change of subject. 'It's not a common name these days. Or maybe in your family it is. You probably have generations of relations called May.'

She took a sip of tea, appearing to think about it.

'There is a first cousin twice removed living in New Zealand, but I don't know of another. People don't have as many children these days. And, since you were listening when I was being interrogated by the paramedics, you must know that I was born in June.'

'I tuned out when they started asking for medical details.'

'Such a gentleman.'

'Such sarcasm.' He gestured at the pergola. 'Besides, the honeysuckle is out now.'

'We've had a warm spring and this one is a bit ahead of itself. It will still be flowering on my birthday. As will the roses. We all have two birth month flowers. When were you born, Lucien?'

'You're going to match me to a flower?'

'It's an old country tradition.'

He rolled his eyes but said, 'September.'

She thought about it for a moment. 'St John's Wort is in flower then.'

'I don't need to ask which of those names you'd choose for me.'

'Don't mock. It's traditionally used for mild depression, poor appetite and trouble sleeping.'

He shifted a little as she touched a sensitive spot. 'You said two flowers.'

'And for September they are the aster—faith, achievement wisdom—also known as Michaelmas daisies.'

'I'll take Michael,' he said with relief.

'And *convolvulus arvensis*. Affection, patience, intimate love.' She paused for a heartbeat. Maybe two. 'Also known as Morning Glory.'

Lucien, mid-gulp, spluttered and coughed. 'Dammit, woman, this God-awful tea just came down my nose!'

He glared at her, but she was pressing her lips tightly together in an effort not to laugh as he mopped his face with the hem of his T-shirt. And then he was laughing too.

'You are something else.'

'And what would that be?'

Before he could answer, she grabbed his arm, pointing at a small, dark shape flitting across the garden against the fading lavender sky.

'Is that…?'

'It is. Be very quiet,' she whispered, 'and you'll hear them clicking.'

They watched in silence as the little bats skimmed the garden using echo location in their hunt for insects and moths.

'Have there been a lot of women?' she asked after a while. 'Who are afraid of bats?'

'A few. One…' He shrugged. 'I have no idea if Charlotte was afraid of bats, but I do know that she was scared of my job and hated the fact that I was away more than at home. When it came to a choice—'

'She made you choose?'

'She wanted a family, a partner who was there. It's difficult to be in any kind of serious relationship when you're constantly on the move. Women get hurt.'

'Everyone gets hurt when a relationship ends.'

'That's true, but if I wasn't prepared to give up what I was doing for her I had to accept that I wasn't ready for commitment. In the end, you have to live with yourself, so you keep it casual.'

'But now you're home. Out of danger.'

'Out of danger but a mess. I punched some idiot who was mouthing off racist filth in a bar.'

'That didn't make the ten o'clock news. Or social media,' she added.

'He was smart enough to realise that he was the one who'd look bad, and my friends covered for me, but there comes a time when you know it's over.'

'That's it? There's no going back?'

'I've been seeing a counsellor, but the truth is that I've seen too much and I'm not in any shape to inflict myself on anyone. What about you?' he asked.

'No women.' He didn't laugh. 'One man. A long time ago,' she said, as if the words had been dragged from her. 'When he died in a plane crash, something inside me died too.'

He couldn't think of a thing to say. *I'm sorry* would be meaningless. To his relief, Banks appeared out of the bushes and stood in front of the bench, staring up at him.

'Your cat hates me.'

'He's not that emotional,' Honey explained, clearly as relieved as he was to be back on safe ground. 'He's just letting you know that you're sitting in his spot and expects you to move.'

'Dogs have much better manners, but Banks can have his bench. I have a chapter to kick into shape,' he said, standing up and offering her his hand. 'I'll see you safely inside.'

Honey would have stayed out longer to watch the stars light up, but she knew that if she didn't go in Lucien would insist on staying, or fret about her tripping over the uneven paving and lying injured until she was discovered in the early hours by the milkman.

A small sound escaped her, something between a groan and a sigh.

'Did you say something?'

'No. I was just thinking about my aunt here on her own with no one to see her safely inside. She always seemed indestructible, but I wasn't looking hard enough, and she never said a word...'

'My mother hid her cancer from me. It was a neighbour who found my number and called to tell me I had to get home.'

'Did you make it in time?'

'I had a few days with her. Time to say the things that had to be said. You?'

'Transport was difficult...' She looked up at him. 'Does it ever go away? The guilt?'

'No, but it helps a little if you keep telling yourself that they took pride in our achievements. That it was what they wanted for us. And they knew they were loved,' he said, as he helped her to her feet. He continued to hold her until he was sure she had her balance.

'But it's what we do that matters.'

'I'm sure she knew that what you were doing was important, Honey.'

He handed her the crutches, then put a steadying hand on her back as they headed slowly towards the door, ready to catch her if she tripped on the uneven paving.

It should have been irritating. She was perfectly capable of walking a few yards without falling on her face. No one had ever treated her as if she was fragile, even when it felt as if she were shattering into a million tiny pieces...

Lucien added the mugs to the dishwasher, then glanced at her.

'The tabs are under the sink.'

He found them and turned it on. 'Do you need a hand with the stairs?'

'There's an *en suite* bedroom on the ground floor.'

'For your aunt?'

'She had it installed for her father but gave it a very classy makeover when she decided to move downstairs. I'll be very comfortable.'

'You've got your painkillers where you can find them?'

She nodded.

'What about another ice pack?'

'Don't fuss, Lucien. I can manage.'

'Of course you can,' he said, but he didn't move, and she suspected that it was less about concern for her than reluctance to go back to the dark and empty Dower House, where the echoes of a war that haunted him were waiting. 'Thanks for…'

'The bats?' she offered when he hesitated.

'The bats were special,' he agreed, grabbing at something impersonal. 'But I've got five thousand words to write, and you need to sleep.'

'You're going to work now?'

'I'm going to try,' he said, finally making it to the door.

'Lucien…'

He stopped and half turned, his expression so intense that her words remained unsaid in her throat.

For long seconds they were frozen in that moment, before he spun round and walked swiftly back to her, taking her face between his hands.

She could feel the roughness of his scarred palms against her cheeks, smell the warmth coming off his body, musky, masculine, overlain with the head-clearing scent of the rosemary growing in the frog by the door.

But her senses were overridden, consumed by the intensity of his gaze, and when he breathed her name, every syllable of Honeysuckle Rose a question, she forgot what she had been going to say and closed her eyes.

Her pulse beat once, twice, before, with a raw, desperate groan, his mouth came down on hers with a fierceness that carried her back until she was stopped by the curved door of the vintage fridge with only his body, the bones and the heat of him holding her upright.

Her crutches hit the floor with a crash, her fingers digging into his shoulders as he leaned into her, drinking in his kiss like water in a desert.

It took her breath, stopped her heart, turned her centre to liquid heat, and she gave it back with all the passion she'd been hoarding for years.

Lucien was the first to recover his senses, leaning his forehead against hers while he caught his breath.

'Honey…'

He was holding her so close that there was no disguising his physical response. He was going to apologise for that, or the kiss. She heard it in the agonised way he'd said her name, and she couldn't bear it.

'Don't!' He lifted his head, searching her face. 'It's been a strange day,' she said before he said it, or something very like it. The kind of excuses men made when they'd done something that they immediately regretted and were desperate to escape. 'And those words won't write themselves.'

He continued to look at her for what felt like a lifetime, then took a step back.

Without his body to hold her against the fridge door, she was in danger of sliding into a crumpled heap at his feet, and she grabbed for the handle the second he bent to pick up her crutches.

'Honey,' he began, but she cut him off.

'I know. Casual.'

'The word I had in mind was "unforgettable",' he said, handing her the crutches before he turned and left without looking back.

Honey, released from the effort of appearing to be completely in control, from the effects of that mind-blowing kiss, was finally able to sink onto the nearest chair. That was when she discovered that it wasn't only her legs that were trembling but her entire body.

Exhilarated. Afraid…

She drew in a long, shuddering breath, laid her head on her arms and waited for her heartbeat to settle back into its normal steady rhythm.

She was still struggling with that when her phone, lying beside her bleeped to let her know she had a text.

Lucien was all but running by the time he reached Honey's gate, only slowing once he'd heard the catch snap into place.

A safety barrier.

It had been there from the moment he'd spotted her on the boat house deck. The insults and the banter were a kind of foreplay, a disguise for the sexual tension, there from that moment on his doorstep when anger could so easily have spilled over into hot, mindless sex.

Casual…

That kiss hadn't felt like any casual encounter

he'd ever known. And now he knew for certain that it had happened before. That he hadn't been dreaming or imagining that he'd kissed her on his doorstep.

He'd felt it, known it somewhere deep in his gut, but had been controlling it until she'd said his name in a way that had bypassed his brain and gone straight to his...

He stopped and cursed himself for an idiot.

He'd been on the point of leaving when she'd thought of something she needed and called him back. The rest was all in his head. What he wanted to hear...

He took out his phone but, reluctant to risk the intimacy of her voice in his ear until he'd had a long, cold shower, he opted for the safety of a text.

Honey, I'm sorry...

He deleted that. Told himself to keep it brief and to the point.

You called me back just as I was leaving, Honey. Was there something else you needed? L

He contemplated adding a kiss. Rejected the idea immediately and deleted the 'else', which might just come across as a little passive aggressive. 'Else' would imply that she'd asked for the kiss. She hadn't, but he could still feel where her fingers had dug into his shoulders as she'd clung on, her mouth hot silk and fully engaged.

And he deleted the 'Honey', which sounded far too much like an endearment.

He clicked 'send' then paced the bank, anticipating a swift reply. He waited long minutes and was about to give up, hoping that she was getting ready for bed rather than ignoring his message, when a beep alerted him to an incoming text.

I just wanted to say that I'll return your sweater when I've washed it. H

Matter-of-fact to the point of brusqueness.

He could hear her saying it in the same calm voice with which she'd reminded him that he had five thousand words to write. As she'd dismissed him with her cool, 'I know.'

For a moment he felt oddly deflated. He didn't know what he'd expected. The spirit, the sharpness of their usual exchanges? The soft, velvet voice that had made his name sound like a sin?

He swore at his own stupidity.

That hadn't been the voice of a woman thinking about laundry. A woman who, despite the composure with which she'd sent him back to his desk, had clutched at the fridge door handle for support, barely able to stand after the kind of mindblowing kiss that should only ever have ended up in one place.

She hadn't ignored his text. It had taken her that long to think of a convincing answer to the question...

Forget the cold shower.

He stripped off, waded out into the river and dived beneath the surface before he was the one hammering on her door and calling out her lie.

CHAPTER EIGHT

'...*rosemary, growing by the door, allows only love to enter.*'
—Traditional

IT HAD TAKEN Honey frantic minutes to come up with a convincing answer to Lucien's text.

For most of that time she'd been kidding herself that she hadn't known what she'd wanted when she'd said his name.

He'd seemed so reluctant to leave and the thought had come to her that she should ask him to stay. Not because she needed help, but because he looked as if he did. There was plenty of room...

Still lying to herself.

Her body had been tingling ever since that moment on his front doorstep. Craving attention. The touch of a man's hand. His hand...

He'd said there were no serious relationships, but Jenny Logan had given him the keys to her four-by-four for just one reason. She wasn't down on the farm counting sheep. She was counting the days until he drove it back to her. It might be a forlorn hope that he was ready to settle down, but they had history. He'd feel safe with her.

Not that she'd been thinking of Jenny when Lucien's tongue had been blazing the way to a deeper intimacy, the soft ache of desire stoked to fever pitch but left unsatisfied.

She re-read his text.

You called me back just as I was leaving. Was there something you needed? L

Not answering was out of the question. He'd think there was a problem and within minutes he'd be back, fishing the key from beneath the frog to let himself in. All it would take was one look and he'd know how much she wanted him.

This was new, terrifying, a risk that she wasn't ready to take. She fastened her hand around her forget-me-not tattoo, digging her nails in to keep herself grounded.

The flower was supposed to alleviate grief, but it had become a reminder that everyone she had ever loved had been taken from her, and there was only so much pain one person could take.

She had to answer him…

He'd kept it impersonal and she must do the same.

Casting around for something, anything, she thought of the lasagne dish that she'd have to return, then saw his sweater lying on the arm of the sofa.

She thumbed in a brisk text that matched his matter-of-fact tone and hit send.

She'd wash the sweater and give it to the postman to drop in at the Dower House, along with Alma's dish. No more dicing with her dangerously attractive neighbour.

Unfortunately, her body wasn't on the same wavelength as her head and was still jangling with frustrated desire. Knowing that she wouldn't sleep, she went back outside to watch the moon rise against the darkening sky. And, because it had become chilly, she picked up Lucien's sweater to drape around her shoulders. She breathed in his scent one last time.

She had just reached the bench when she heard a splash.

Brian had told her that a pair of otters had been spotted on the Hart and, confident on her crutches now, she swung quickly down the garden to the gate.

There was something in the water swimming beneath the surface, and she held her breath, wishing she'd had the sense to bring her phone with her so that she could take a photograph when it broke the surface.

Which was when history repeated itself.

Except that, unlike her aunt, she wasn't ten years old, and the naked man rising from the depths of the river wasn't a royal prince who was about to cause a constitutional crisis.

Lucien was facing downriver towards the boat house, and, by the time he turned to step up onto the bank she had backed deep into the bushes.

She was hidden from view but unable to move without betraying her presence, although her heart was hammering so hard it was a miracle that he didn't hear it.

He stood on the bank for what felt like an age, his wet skin silvered by the moon, the shadows highlighting bone and muscle.

Honey froze as he glanced towards the gate, then smiled and said, 'Rosemary.'

What?

The man barely knew a daisy from a buttercup, but the air was filled with the scent of the rosemary that had been growing by the garden gate for as long as she could remember. He must have brushed against it as he left. Or maybe she had as she'd taken cover.

He shook the water from his hair, then scooped up his discarded clothes. She was forced to watch as, with shoes dangling from the fingers of one hand, clothes in the other, he walked barefoot and buck naked along the path until he was out of sight.

It was the sun lighting up the corner of the room as it rose above the trees that made Lucien look up.

He blinked, rubbed his face and sat back, astonished to discover that it was nearly six o'clock and he'd been writing all night.

He stood up, stretched out limbs that had barely

moved since he'd showered off his plunge in the river, pulled on fresh running gear and, as he and sleep were not on speaking terms, headed for his desk.

He'd told Honey that he had five thousand words to write. He'd done that and more and, for the first time since he'd yielded to pressure from his agent to write a book about his experiences.

He picked up his phone, checking in case Honey had sent a text, but there was nothing.

Which should have been a relief.

Was a relief...

There was something unsettling in the way she managed to tease things out of him and made him confront things that he'd hidden from both his counsellor and Jenny. His father's desertion, the memory lapses...

He grabbed a bottle of water and set off for a run. He took a detour via the boat house to take some photographs of the damage to send to the letting agent, along with a report of the accident and a demand that it was made safe.

That done, he began to walk rather than run along the towpath. He stopped to look at the fritillaries that had caught Honey's attention, drank some water then carried on at the same pace, keeping an eye out for the ducklings.

As he approached Honey's gate, he became aware of the clack of shears being wielded with vigour and the occasional expletive muttered in a familiar voice. He paused to brush his hand over the soft new growth of the rosemary bush that he'd noticed the night before.

It released a head-clearing rush of scent and Honey immediately stopped what she was doing.

She was half hidden behind a tall shrub that was bearing the brunt of her shears but, if she was hoping to remain unnoticed, she was about to be disappointed.

Her dress—a green print that was the same colour as the grass—might be long enough to cover her to her feet but the neckline scooped low to reveal an enticing hint of the treasure beneath. And it fastened all the way down the front with large cream buttons that had been designed to give a man ideas.

'Rosemary,' he said. 'According to Shakespeare, it's for remembrance. '

'According to Delia Smith,' she replied, 'it's for roast lamb.'

He frowned. There was a distinct edge to her voice. Honey was clearly annoyed at having been discovered being a very bad patient. Or was it embarrassment at her response to last night's kiss?

'I prefer mint with lamb,' he said.

'"Plant mint for virtue, marjoram for joy, sage for wisdom, thyme for courage and myrtle…"'

She began to hack viciously at the bush.

'Myrtle?'

'I can't remember the rest of it.'

'That bang on the head, probably,' he sympathised, but not believing her for a minute. 'You're up early.'

'I'm a lark. What's your excuse?'

That was better. More like the Honey he found so very…stimulating.

'I haven't been to bed. Does that make me an owl?'

She lowered the shears and finally turned to look at him. From the shadows beneath her eyes, he rather thought the early start was due to a poor night's sleep.

'That's a bit extreme, even for an owl,' she said with what sounded very like concern. 'Those five thousand words must have been highly stimulating.'

'It was a different five thousand words that kept me awake. I decided to junk everything I'd written so far and start again.'

'And you've still got the energy for a run?'

'I feel a lot better now I'm on the right track. It must have been the camomile tea. But it's probably going to be a walk today.'

'Good decision. Take care not to nod off and fall in.'

He would have sworn that Honeysuckle Rose didn't know how to blush, but a tinge of pink flushed her neck as she turned away, taking a little more care with her clipping.

'Should you be doing that?'

'Forsythia has to be cut back after flowering or it gets leggy.'

'I'm not interested in the plant life. It's your foot that concerns me. How is it today?'

'Ice pack applied, pain killers and antibiotics taken.'

'But not propped up.' He opened the gate and held out a hand for the shears. 'Hand them over.'

'Lucien!' He waited. 'If I don't do it now, it will still look twiggy on open day.'

'Then tell me what to do and I'll finish it.'

'Oh, but—'

'I'm not a gardener, but you're cutting back a bush with outsize scissors while balanced on one foot. How hard can it be?'

A little huff of outrage escaped her lips, but she finally surrendered the shears. 'I've done most of it, but I can't put enough weight on my foot to reach the top.'

'How much would you like me to chop off?'

'Half a metre?'

'I think I can manage that.' He nodded at a wheelbarrow waiting for the clippings that were piled up around her feet. 'And the debris?'

'Follow the path beside the glasshouse and you'll come to a yard with a row of compost bins.'

He nodded, hefted the shears to get the balance and then began to chop away the top growth.

Honey didn't move and he stopped. 'I'm doing this so that you can go and put your foot up,

Honey. I'll come and make you whatever con-coction you desire when this is done.'

He didn't wait for her to argue but carried on cutting, and the next time he glanced back he was alone.

He made short work of the job, gathered up the mound of clippings and headed for the yard where he tipped them into a half-empty compost bin.

Then he took out his phone and put as much as he could remember of that quote about herbs into the search engine. Nothing came up, but a sec-ond check on "myrtle" informed him that it was an evergreen shrub with glossy, aromatic foliage and white flowers, that they were always used in royal wedding bouquets and meant good luck and love in marriage.

He frowned. Why would Honey hesitate to say that? She'd said there had been a man a long time ago, who'd been killed. Had they been married.?

Was it myrtle tattooed around her wrist?

He looked again at the picture. No. Those flow-ers had a much simpler shape and were blue. There were some very like it growing in the amongst the long grass.

'Honey?' There was a tap on the back door. 'Jack saw the ambulance leaving the Dower House yes-terday, and of course we were all agog, but then we discovered that it wasn't Lucien Grey but you…'

Honey blinked, struggling to focus. 'Oh, hi,

Diana. I must have dropped off for a moment. Come in.'

The invitation was unnecessary. Her visitor had already plumped herself down on the pouffe.

'Who told you I'd had an accident?' she asked.

'Sally Wickes. Do you know her? Her husband opened the bakery a couple of years ago.'

'We've met.'

'Well, they found your watch in the X-ray department after you'd left yesterday, and Sally's mother works in the office at the hospital, so she offered to return it to you.'

'So why didn't she?'

'She had the grandchildren last night, so she left it with Sally. When I called in this morning and heard you were laid up, I offered to bring it over.' She grinned as she produced it from her bag. 'The village grapevine is in full working order. I brought you a loaf too. And a couple of blueberry muffins, as the croissants were still too hot. They're on the kitchen table.'

'That's really thoughtful. Exactly what I need. My purse is in my basket.'

'Don't be silly. I didn't want to come empty-handed to the sick bed, but bringing you flowers is like shipping sand to the Sahara.'

'Well, thank you.' She glanced at her phone. 'I appear to have quite a few missed calls.'

'You know how it is. So? What happened?'

'It was just a stupid accident. I was on the path

by the river when I noticed that the boat house is in a really bad state so, like an idiot, I went to take a closer look.'

'And?'

'And my foot went through a rotten board. There's a bit of damage to my heel from some rotten wood and I've sprained my ankle rather badly.'

'Ouch! Thank goodness for mobile phones, or who knows how long you'd have been lying there? It's not as if your neighbour ever leaves the house, and Alma's away…' Torn between defending Lucien and preserving his privacy, Honey decided that he'd much prefer the latter and said nothing. 'How are you managing?'

'I've got the crutches under control, but I'm supposed to keep my foot elevated for a day or two, which is why you find me lying on the sofa on such a lovely morning instead of in the garden, getting things ready for the open day.'

'Oh, Lord, that's quite soon, isn't it?'

'The third weekend.'

'We were actually wondering if you were going ahead with it this year. We've seen so little of you since you came home.'

'I needed some time, Diana.'

'We all understand. Flora's death, and Alma said you haven't been well… Now this. Will you have to cancel?'

'Cancel?'

Diana blinked at the sound of a man's voice

and then her jaw sagged as she saw Lucien, in his shorts and a running vest, filling the doorway. While he'd clearly lost weight, every bit of softness from his body, there was no missing his wide, sinewy shoulders or the ropey muscles on his upper arms and thighs.

'Mr Grey.'

'The summer fete lady…' He frowned, clearly searching for a name. 'Mrs Marks?' he hazarded.

'Mrs Markham chairs the village fete committee,' Honey said, as Diana, uncharacteristically, seemed to have lost the power of speech. 'And she runs the antique shop in the village with her sister.'

'Of course. You left a card.' He came forward, hand outstretched but saw it was smeared with green sap from the new young leaves of the bush he'd been cutting back. 'Perhaps not,' he said, wiping it down his vest.

'Mr Grey saw me struggling with a pair of shears when he was on his morning run on the towpath, Diana,' Honey explained. 'And came to my rescue.'

'Did he?' It came out as a squeak. 'How kind.'

'One good turn. Honey stitched me up when I had a close encounter with some shrapnel in Syria.'

'Oh, but that's such a coincidence,' she said. And then clearly wondered if it was. 'But how naughty of you to be working in the garden when you should be resting your foot, Honey. You know you only have to ask and we'd all help.'

'That's exactly what I told her, Mrs Markham,'

Lucien said, his face poker-straight. 'I'm about to make us both a drink. Will you join us? Tea, coffee?'

Honey rolled her eyes in exasperation at him. She'd been doing her best to keep their acquaintance to the level of a good turn from a passing neighbour…

Honey saw Diana struggle between wanting to stay and her desperation to get back to the village with the news that Lucien Grey was out of hibernation and the *You'll never guess where he's making himself at home* gossip…

'Thank you, Mr Grey, but I can't stay,' she said, gossip trumping coffee. 'It's my day to open the shop, but I called in to return Honey's watch and, since I was in the bakery, bring her some sustaining carbs.'

'Village life,' Lucien said. 'So supportive.'

'We like to think so,' Diana replied, never taking her eyes off him as she backed towards the door. 'We've missed you, Honey. If you need anything…'

'I'll call you. And thanks again for the bread and muffins.'

Neither of them spoke until they heard her footsteps speeding across the gravel drive.

'Is she actually running?' Lucien asked.

'With phone in hand, I imagine. You're going to have to hammer boards across your front door now that you've been spotted in the wild.'

'I'm more worried that there'll be a back door key hidden under a flowerpot.'

'Do you have a bolt?' Honey lifted her shoulders in an apologetic shrug. 'I'm sorry, but you only have yourself to blame. I made no mention of nettles, your part in the accident or your gallant three hours in the hospital waiting room. Then you ruined it all by offering her a drink.'

'I was hoping she'd ask for coffee so that I could join her, rather than have some herbal concoction foisted on me. And you appear to have forgotten that I brought you dinner,' he said. 'And rescued your plants.'

'I haven't forgotten a thing…' Feeling her cheeks heat up, she shook her head, realising that it was a conversation heading for trouble. 'I'm just sorry that your kind gesture has exposed you to speculation.'

'I doubt you fell through that rotten board with the sole purpose of making my life difficult, so stop apologising.'

'Only *doubt*?' she asked because, while her head was full of remorse for having laid him open to village gossip, her mouth hadn't caught up. 'You're not certain?'

'The only things in life I'm certain of are death and taxes. And the fact that you are trouble. Now, if it's okay with you, I'm going to clean up and then I'll put the kettle on.'

CHAPTER NINE

'Rest is not idleness, and to lie sometimes on the grass under trees on a summer's day, listening to the murmur of the water, or watching the clouds float across the sky, is by no means a waste of time.'
—*The Use of Life*, John Lubbock

LUCIEN SPENT RATHER longer washing his hands than was strictly necessary, but he needed a minute after that exchange to compose himself.

The reflection looking back at him suggested it was going to take a lot longer than that, but when he couldn't put it off any longer he found Honey standing in front of the fridge, examining its contents.

'I can't take my eyes off you for a minute!'

Unabashed, she continued to survey the contents of the fridge. 'Was it Mark Twain who said that nothing improves the view like ham and eggs? Or in this case, the more portable option of a bacon sandwich.'

'Portable?' he repeated as she removed a pack of bacon and a butter dish from the fridge.

'I thought we might have breakfast in the orchard.' She nudged the door closed with her shoulder. 'Unless, of course, you had breakfast at some unearthly hour, in which case it would be a mid-morning snack.'

'It's nowhere near mid-morning.'

'That rather depends on when you started your day. In your case it could be any meal you care to name. Shall we settle on breakfast?'

'Whatever you say.'

'My three favourite words,' she said, rewarding him with a smile. 'Remember them. In the mean-time, you know where to find the kettle, and you'll find a couple of mugs in the cupboard.'

'Honey…'

But she was already at the stove, laying slices of bacon into a pan, and he didn't waste his breath telling her to go back to the sofa and leave it to him. She was the nurse. Presumably she knew what her foot could take.

He filled the kettle, found the mugs and put some coffee in the cafetière. Honey raised an eye-brow, but she didn't say anything.

'Is there something else I can do?' he asked.

'Cut the bread?'

He located the breadboard, found a knife that suited him, sharpened it on a steel and cut four slices from the warm loaf.

'Oh, you're a keeper,' Honey said as he spread the butter without tearing it 'I just mean that I'd have ended up with mess of crumbs,' she added, all uncharacteristic blushing confusion.

'You need a sharp knife,' he said, doing his best

to keep a straight face. Having found some tomatoes, he sliced them, then went out to the glasshouse to pick salad leaves.

The door and roof lights were open; everything smelled fresh and green. It was a calm space and he could easily spend a day in there working. All he needed was the right chair and his laptop...

Casual, he decided, could become his least favourite word. He pushed the thought away—he was in no state to offer anything more—and back in the kitchen he concentrated on rinsing and drying the leaves.

'Is the bacon ready?' he asked.

'It is.'

'Then I'll leave you to fill the mugs while I construct the sandwiches.'

'Only a man would treat a sandwich as a construction project.'

'Only a woman would suggest it was anything else,' he said, then smiled at her, so she'd know that he wasn't being serious.

Whatever smart remark she'd been about to come back with died in her throat and long seconds passed as they just looked at one another. Sandwiches were the last thing on either of their minds.

Damn, this was a mistake. He should have kept walking...

'Bacon,' she said, passing him the pan, before

turning away to fill the mugs, giving them both a moment to catch their breath.

'Your BLT, ma'am,' he said.

'You're a bit of a ham yourself,' she shot back, putting lids on the mugs, taking a clean tea cloth from a drawer and wrapping the sandwiches. 'Can you carry everything?'

He caught the handles of the two mugs in one hand and picked up the sandwiches while Honey scribbled a note to stick on the door.

'"With the bees"?'

'Now you've been spotted looking very much at home here, I'm going to get more visitors. If I don't answer, they'll let themselves in, using the excuse that they're checking to make sure I haven't fallen and done myself more damage. And, if they don't find me, they'll come looking.'

'But not if you're with your bees.'

'Would you?'

'I might sit on the bench and wait for you.'

'In your case it would be guilt, not gossip.'

'I have nothing to feel guilty about,' he protested.

'So why are you here? Helping in the garden. Making coffee and sandwiches.'

He had no answer to that, at least not one that he wanted to think about. 'As I said to Mrs Summer Fete, village life is supportive. I fear it may be catching.'

'Unavoidable. She'll have you in her sights now,

Lucien. You should get back to London before she has you signed up for the tombola.'

'London. Where nobody knows your name.' Why had that ever seemed such an attractive idea? 'I had planned to rent somewhere until my flat became vacant, but I wasn't in a great place when I arrived back in England. People were worried about me being on my own.'

'Because of the flashbacks? The panic attacks?'

He stopped. For a moment everything had felt calm, comfortable, and now he felt exposed, vulnerable, wanting to drop everything and run...

As if she sensed it, she let go of a crutch and put her hand on his arm, as if to hold him still. It was nothing, no more than a touch, and yet it felt like everything...

'You know.' He shook his head. 'Stupid. Of course you know. You've been there, you've seen it. You saw what happened to me when you came to the door brandishing those nettles and I did recognise you. I don't mean that I knew who you were, just that on some subconscious level I knew we'd met. That it had been important.' He looked down at her hand on his arm. It was small, but exuded strength... 'You held my arm then too. You're always there, holding my arm when I need it.'

'I should have done more, and afterwards I was ashamed that I hadn't, but I was so angry...' She gave a little hiccupping sob, and in a heartbeat she was the one needing the prop. 'I've been angry for so long…'

He knew how she felt—the rage, the utter helplessness—and, although his hands were full, he put his arms around her. For a moment she resisted, but then she gave it up, laying her head against his shoulder as he gathered her close.

For a while they stood there, drenched in the scent of apple blossom, while above them a blackbird sang his heart out.

'You need to talk about it, Honey.'

She lifted her head and looked at him. 'Is that what you were told?' she asked, answering a question with a question. She did a lot of that, but he needed to earn her trust. He picked up the fallen crutch and handed it to her.

'I was told that writing is useful,' he said, as they continued to make their way slowly through the trees.

'Writing, maybe, but I don't think you should be listening to your diaries, reliving your experiences every waking moment.'

'No?' He glanced at her. 'What would you prescribe, Sister Rose?'

'I understand that servicemen suffering from PTSD find being out in the open air, doing practical things with their hands, helpful.'

'Gardening?'

'It heals the heart.'

They were deep in the orchard now. The blackbird had followed them, keeping up his challenge. There was a soft buzz from bees working amongst the blossom but the rest was silence.

'Practical help in return for restoration of the soul. It sounds like a good deal to me.'

'Then consider yourself welcome to come and spend time in the garden whenever you like,' she said, heading for the trunk of a fallen tree that had been smoothed to provide a seat. 'I can always find you something to do.'

He handed her one of the mugs, then sat down beside her, unwrapped the sandwiches and offered them to her.

She took one and for a moment they both ate in silence.

'It's so peaceful here.'

'It's my favourite place in the entire world. When things were really tough,' she said, 'I would imagine myself sitting here. The scent, the hum of the bees…'

'The butterflies?' he suggested as one settled on the sleeve of her dress. 'What was Diana Markham talking about when she said you'd have to cancel?'

'The National Garden Open Day. Hundreds of people all over the country open their gardens to visitors for one or two days in the summer.'

'Like stately homes?'

'They don't have to be grand. Most are quite

small, even allotments. Some people open their homes so that people can see their houseplants.'

'You just open your gate—metaphorically in your case—and allow people to wander around?'

'It's a more organised than that. It's for charity so there's a five-pound entry fee. And the WI serves afternoon tea.'

'Cucumber sandwiches and scones with clotted cream and home-made jam?'

'There's a little more choice of sandwiches, and wonderful cakes. With elderflower champagne as an optional extra.'

'Which you have yet to make.'

'I'm sure I can find a teenager to help for a small fee.'

'The way that you used to help your aunt?'

'I didn't expect her to pay me.' Aware that she sounded a little defensive, she added, 'Brian sells plants to visitors and this year, for the first time, I'm going to be the one leading a tour of the pond, the beehives and the meadow. Doing my best to answer their questions. Any children who come along can take part in a bug hunt and pond dipping, and they get a plant to take home and nurture.'

'It sounds very special, but a lot of work.'

'The special makes it worth it.'

'And that's why, instead of keeping your foot up, you were cutting back the forsythia. Because otherwise it would still look twiggy on open day.'

She smiled. 'And now it won't, thanks to you.'

'So, what else will you be hacking down the minute my back is turned?'

'Nothing.'

'I don't believe you.'

'That is so rude.'

'Possibly, but I'm right.' She didn't answer. 'Tell me what I can do to help.'

'You have a book to write, Lucien.'

'One that you don't think I should be writing.'

'It doesn't seem like the best idea right now.'

'Maybe,' he said, 'but I felt I had to get it down on paper. That people had to know. The reality is that I was just spewing my guts on paper. Hoping to get it out of my head.'

Lucien was looking into a distance that no one else could see, and Honey grasped his wrist, anchoring him on the log beside her, safe in the peace of the orchard.

He didn't look at her, but he covered her hand with his own, acknowledging her awareness of his black moment. Reassuring her that he was okay.

'I've decided to take a different angle,' he said. 'One that tells the stories of the men, women and children I've met while I've been reporting from war zones. Their courage, the spirit of endurance. And the people who, in the midst of danger, are doing what they can to help. If the publisher doesn't like it...'

'He will,' she assured him.

'Maybe.' He looked at her then. 'But, if he doesn't, I'll return his advance.'

'You haven't spent it?'

'I've found a use for it, but thanks to Jenny's talent and hard work the production company has done very well. I can cover it.'

Jenny...

Honey extracted her hand from beneath Lucien's and took a bite of a sandwich she was no longer tasting, and she needed a swig of coffee to get down her throat.

'How is the project on her farm going?' she asked.

'Nearly there. One of the networks has bought it and it's lined up for next spring. After that, I'll be taking over,' he said, tossing a small piece of bacon to a tame robin.

'Jenny doesn't mind surrendering the lead after all her hard work?' Honey asked.

'She is taking a much-deserved break. She'll have to put herself out there, do the chat shows when the time comes, but with a baby on the way—'

'A baby?'

Honey felt the colour drain from her face and then Lucien put a hand to her back, steadying her.

'Put your head between your knees. There's no water. Will coffee do?'

'I'm okay...'

'And I'm Dick Robinson. Are you in pain?'

'No,' she snapped. Not the kind of pain that a pill could fix. How dared he kiss her? Not that first time—he'd had no idea what he was doing then—but last night had been different.

She'd wanted it so badly and if she hadn't been running scared…

And today he was back, playing house, and she had been loving it, wanting it, pushing Jenny to the back of her mind.

She shook him off, holding up her hand palm out, to keep him away.

'Don't…'

'Don't what?' he demanded and then, as the penny dropped, 'Dammit, Honey, you can't think…' He took a breath and drew back. 'Clearly you do.'

'She's your partner.'

'Jenny is my *business* partner. It's Saffy, Jenny's wife, who's having the baby.'

'Wife?'

'Their wedding was all over the media last year. I assumed you knew.'

It took a moment for what he was saying to fully sink in and then, overcome with embarrassment, she finally allowed her head sink to her knees.

'I don't know what to say.'

'A win, then,' he said.

Rude, but she was in no position to complain.

On the foot-in-mouth scale, this was up to her patella.

'I'm so sorry...'

'Why don't you sit up, look me in the face and tell me that?' he suggested.

Right at that moment all she wanted was for the ground to open and swallow her. That wasn't about to happen, and mumbling an apology into her skirt wasn't going to fix this. She doubted anything could fix it, but she took a breath, lifted her head, squared her shoulders and turned to him, hoping for the smallest hint of forgiveness.

His face was, apparently, set in stone.

'There are no words...' No reaction. She swallowed. *Keep it brief, keep it simple...* 'I am so sorry, Lucien.'

Nothing changed in his expression for what felt like a lifetime, but then he reached out and cradled her cheeks between his hands.

'I'm not.'

It took a moment for what he was saying to sink in.

She had insulted him, suggesting that he'd be capable of betraying a mother of his baby with meaningless sex. Because sex with any man who could do that had to be meaningless...

And in doing so she had discovered—and betrayed—exactly how meaningful it would have been to her.

He leaned forward and touched his lips to hers in a *Did that actually happen?* kiss.

She had betrayed her feelings and he wasn't sorry. Wasn't he going to run a mile?

'There were rumours,' she said, searching his face, desperate for a hint of what he was feeling. 'Of a romance.'

'And of course you believe everything you read in the red-tops.'

It was her turn to let slip an expletive.

'I'm an idiot.'

He didn't contradict her, just put his arm around her, and somehow her head was on his shoulder.

'Lucien?'

'What?'

'Who's Dick Robinson?'

She felt the rumble of laughter. 'No one. It's just an expression my mother used when I told her something she thought was improbable.'

'Such as?'

'That I'd cleaned my shoes, done my homework, tidied my room.'

'Aunt Flora didn't have to say a word. She'd just look at me over the top of her glasses and I was gone.' She sighed. 'At the time, you're all moody teenage "it's not fair". You only learn to value those moments when they're just a memory.'

'What are you going to do, Honey?' His gesture took in the garden, the orchard and the cottage. 'Once I've written the book,' he said, 'I'll be commissioning and producing television series. Will you stay here and pick up the flag of conservation? Or will you be going back overseas?'

She shook her head.

'No.' She began to break pieces of bread off her sandwich, tossing them to the sparrows. 'After Aunt Flora died I wasn't sleeping, wasn't eating. In truth, my breakdown had probably been creeping up on me for a long time before that, but I finally cracked at the end of February. You think I was angry over the caterpillars? Believe me, it was nothing to how I reacted when a water pump froze.'

She'd known it for weeks but had been in denial. Saying it out loud made it a fact.

'But that doesn't rule out nursing here at home, does it?'

'I've lost my confidence, Lucien. The thought of being responsible for anyone's life fills me with terror. All I have ahead of me is a great big void with nothing to fill it with but making elderflower champagne.'

'Don't forget the dandelions,' he said in an effort to make her smile.

'You have to pick an awful lot of dandelions...' Her voice was shaking as the reality hit and he caught her hand, holding it steady. Holding her steady, as a few minutes ago she had held him...

'A whole gallon of petals, so I've heard.'

'You remembered.'

'When you talked about making it with your aunt,' he said, 'it sounded as if it really mattered to you.'

'It did. It does. But it's hardly a career.'

He was looking at her and it was there again. A repeat of that split second in the cottage before he'd kissed her. A life-changing moment when anything might happen.

Not now.

If he kissed her now it would be out of pity and she turned away.

'You have a beautiful home, a garden you're clearly passionate about. Maybe that should be your starting point?' he suggested.

'It's not mine.' She pulled her hand away. 'None of this is mine. This is Flora's garden and I don't know nearly enough.'

'You can learn if it matters to you,' he said. 'But she wouldn't have wanted her legacy to make you unhappy.'

'Then she shouldn't have left me.'

She waved the words away before he could offer her comfort. Or counselling. Who was the one with a problem now?

'Oh, wait… I get it,' she rattled on before he could say anything. 'You think I should set up as the local hedge witch, doling out potions made from the herbs in Aunt Flora's…sorry, *my*…garden?'

'Well, that's one option…and she clearly had a very good life.'

CHAPTER TEN

*'Yet soon fair Spring shall give another scene.
And yellow cowslips gild the level green.'*
—Anne E Bleecher

THE MINUTE THE words were out of his mouth,
Lucien knew he'd made a mistake. Honey had
been back on the defensive, blanking out a future
that seemed to offer her nothing, and he'd fallen
into the trap.

Having experienced an up close and personal
experience of her blowing her top, he prepared to
duck. For long seconds they both held their breath
and then she swallowed hard and began taking the
slow, measured breaths that he recognised from
his own sessions with a therapist.

'Professor Flora Rose,' she said, when she was
sufficiently in control to speak, 'was a botanist
who travelled the world until she found herself
saddled with a six-year-old orphan at an age when
most women would be retiring. Not that she ever
retired.'

'Professor…?'

He'd thought he was in trouble. This was trouble tripled…

'Alma didn't mention that when you were having your little *tête-à-tête* about the crazy woman

next door?' she asked with that edge of sarcasm that made any conversation with Honey such a dangerously enticing game.

'I asked her for your name so that I could send a note, apologising for the way I spoke to you. Nothing else.'

'Oh, dear…' She shook her head but, as quickly as it had come, the tension seeped from her body, her voice. 'Poor Lucien. You asked a simple question and got a history lesson.'

'Pretty much.' At the time he'd wanted to escape. Now he wished he'd taken more notice. 'She told me that your aunt was responsible for all the wildflowers and butterflies in the village.'

'Her re-wilding project didn't meet with universal approval, but it's become something of a model for other places, and now it brings visitors to study, as well as enjoy, what has been done here. And that, of course, has proved beneficial for the local economy.'

'Like Diana Markham's antique shop?'

'Like the antique shop, the book shop and the boutique that sells locally made crafts and New Agey stuff,' she confirmed. 'And the Hartford Arms does a roaring trade in lunches.'

'Creating jobs,' he said. 'Keeping young people in the village.'

'All that,' she agreed.

'She sounds like quite a woman.'

She gave a little sigh and he wanted to hold her,

as he had when they'd walked into the orchard, but he sensed that this was the wrong moment to do anything but listen.

'Your arrival was clearly a life-changing moment for her,' he prompted. 'How did she cope with a grieving six-year-old?'

'With kindness and the peaceful aura that touched everything she did. But, while my arrival might have kept her at home, it didn't slow her down. She continued to write books and articles, lectured to students who adored her and was honoured for her work. The present Prince of Wales was an admirer, and she ended her days as Emeritus Professor in Biodiversity at Melchester University.'

'I had no idea. The wilding, the stillroom, the herbs…' He stopped making excuses and was rewarded with a smile. The kind that came with a kicker. 'What?'

'She was an academic, Lucien, but you're right. She may also have been just a little bit of a hedge witch.'

He laughed out loud at that. 'You're the witch, Honeysuckle Rose, but you've got a lot to live up to.'

'I'd have had to be a second Florence Nightingale to get even close.'

'You've done more than most. You told me that you always wanted to be a nurse, like your mother, but you need to be thinking about the future. What did your father do?'

'He was a Rose,' she said, as if that was answer enough. 'He was working as a consultant on the restoration of a "lost garden". They made a television series about it. I have it on an old VHS tape that has been viewed so often that I'm afraid to play it any more in case it snaps.'

'If you'll trust me with it,' he said. 'I'll get it transferred onto digital for you.'

Her face was transformed by a smile. 'Can you do that?'

'Yes, but clearly it's very precious, so I'll give it to a professional.'

'Thank you.'

He picked up his coffee and for a while they sat in silence while the bolder sparrows came close enough to grab crumbs.

'You come from a family who cherished the earth, Honey,' he said, after a while. 'There's a huge need for that and, sad though it is, you are now the Rose at Orchard End. Perhaps this is the moment to accept your heritage.'

'I am not going to agricultural college.'

'No?' He grinned. 'I can so see you in your dungarees and headscarf, driving a tractor.'

'Stick around. There's a vintage tractor in the stables that comes out for hayrides at the village fete. Say you'll open it, and I'll let you drive it.'

'Tempting as that is…'

'I could call Diana right now. It would do wonders for the fundraising, especially if we offered selfies with the famous Lucien Grey for a small consideration?'

Her wide grin and those warm, sweet lips were the only things tempting him.

'Thanks, but I'll pass. Nice try at changing the subject, though.'

Her look suggested that she hadn't given up hope, but he refused to play.

'You have a science background,' he persisted. 'There must be a wide range of post-grad conservation and bio-diversity courses available. And rewilding is big news these days. With your knowledge, your background…' He didn't push it. 'Or, if you can't work face to face with patients, you could teach.'

She pulled a face.

'Honey, sweetheart, you've tried being your mother and been brilliant. Maybe it's time to start from scratch, go back to the hopes and dreams of that little girl before her life was changed by a traffic accident. It's time to find yourself,' he said, getting to his feet and tossing away the dregs of his coffee. 'But not right now. Right now there's a more pressing problem.'

She looked up at him, a frown creasing the space between eyes that had been all he'd seen of her that first time: dark blue eyes that had stayed in his memory.

'You were going to pick elderflowers today. For the champagne.'

'Now who's changing the subject?' she asked, those eyes huge and dark in the shade of the apple trees.

Tempting, tempting…

'Not at all. Just giving you time to think.'

'While I pick elderflowers? Was that an offer of help, Mr Grey?'

'It was but, unlike the village teenagers, I'll expect my payment in kind, Miss Rose. Two bottles?' he suggested, before there was any chance of a misunderstanding.

'You mean it?' she asked and, as she searched his face, he realised how important it was to her.

'Outside in the fresh air. Doing something practical with my hands. Sister Rose's orders, and right now I think she could do with a little of her own medicine.'

'I…' She shook her head. 'You're undoubtedly right, but not today. You haven't slept for twenty-four hours, and I need to sterilise everything and stock up on lemons and sugar before we start.'

We…

How long had it been since he'd used that word? With Jenny, but that had been business. This was something else. Something that was definitely not casual. It had only been a couple of days, but she had been there in his head for a long time.

'You're not planning on walking to the village, I hope?'

'If I said yes, would you insist on going for me?'

He wanted to tell her to stop. That she didn't have to wear a mask with him.

'There's a limit to my altruism,' he replied, following her lead and keeping it light, a little mocking. 'But I'm sure that if you phone the shop with your smallest need right now, you'll be inundated with offers to deliver.'

Her laughter was his reward.

'You are too smart, Lucien. And just a touch cynical.'

'Smart enough to accept that I need a couple of hours' sleep or I'm going to fall over. As for cynical, right now I'd bet my right arm that texts are flying all over the village and we're the subject of hot gossip in the Post Office queue.'

'Do you mind?'

'Do you?' he asked, realising that he hadn't thought of her, only himself. 'When I realised you had company, I should have made a discreet exit. I'm sorry if I've embarrassed you.'

'You were being kind, Lucien. If people choose to make something of it, that's their problem. Don't give it another thought,' she said. 'Go and catch up on your sleep.'

'If I leave, can I trust you to go inside and rest your foot?'

'I'll certainly rest my foot. Take this and put it

on your pillow,' she said, leaning down to pick a flower, a cluster of small yellow bells, and offering it to him. '*"Where the bee sucks, there suck I. In a cowslip's bell I lie..."* They are said to have a sedative quality.'

She picked another, held it to her nose for a moment and then held out a hand for a lift up.

'I'll walk you back to the cottage.'

'No need. I'm going to lie under that tree and count blossoms until the cowslip and the hum of the bees send me to sleep.'

'*"Merrily, merrily shall I live now",*' he said, continuing her quote, still holding her hand as he supported her to the tree. '*"Under the blossom that hangs on the bough."*'

She smiled. 'You know your Shakespeare.'

'Who knew that English Lit A level would ever be useful?'

'Handy for crosswords.'

He tightened his grip to support her as she lowered herself carefully, her dress blending in with the grass as she settled her skirt around her ankles, one booted, one so slender that he could have circled it with his thumb and forefinger.

'Lucien?' Honey was looking up at him. 'You're going to have to let go of my hand,' she prompted, once she had his attention.

'Or I could take the grass option...?'

He was asking the question. Wanting to stay here with Honey.

'It is so much nicer out in the fresh air than in a stuffy bedroom on a warm, sunny day,' she agreed.

Out in the fresh air, doing something practical with his hands...

He shut down the thought, just grateful to be here as she began to count the blossoms.

'One, two, three...'

The grass was long, soft and threaded with wildflowers. As he stretched out beside her and sank into it, all he could hear was Honey's voice counting slower and slower, 'Twelve...thirteen...' and the soft hum of bees.

Honey was woken by something tickling her cheek. She brushed it away only to discover that it wasn't an insect, but Lucien, with a buttercup, propped on one elbow and watching her.

They were lying outside in the grass, a foot of space between them, and yet the moment had the rare intimacy of that first time waking with a lover.

'You sleep like a baby,' he said. 'Completely open, with no sense of how vulnerable you are, or that the world is full of dangers.'

'The cowslips did their job, then. Did you sleep?' she asked.

'I did, thank you, and for once without dreaming. But now I'm going to take a shower. Are you on for chicken curry tonight?'

'Your place or mine?'

'This is the healing garden,' he replied, leaning across to kiss her cheek. It was no more than a brush of his lips, but it set up the down on her cheeks in a mini-tsunami. 'Do you want a hand up?' he asked, standing up. 'Or are you staying there?'

'Staying,' she managed through what felt like cobwebs. 'No, wait…a hand…'

He grasped both of her hands in his and, once she had her good foot firmly planted, he pulled her upright, taking a step forward and catching her round the waist so that they were touching close.

'Shall I walk you to your door, Honey?'

She sucked in her breath. How could he make such an innocent sentence sound so seductive? How could she be seduced by the sound of his voice?

'N-no… I have to go and talk to the bees.'

That appeared to amuse him. 'Are they good conversationalists?'

'They don't say much, but you have to tell them everything important that's happening in the family.' She discovered that she had to swallow. 'Or they will desert you.'

'When you say everything…'

Lucien had not moved, yet somehow they were closer. So close that he must surely be able to feel how her heart was pounding?

She lifted her hand to place it over his and

found an answering echo. If Lucien had not been holding her, she would have melted at his feet.

Her head was filled with the herby scent of crushed grass and warm skin where he had lain beside her and all she could see was his mouth, the enticing dip of his lower lip just inches from her own...

'When you say *everything*, Honey, will you tell them that I kissed you?'

'I...'

'And will you tell them that you kissed me back?'

Kissed him back, a fully engaged participant, for a moment lost to sense...

'Yes.'

Her mouth formed the word; no sound emerged. It wasn't an answer to his question—not that question, anyway—and Lucien took his time, searching her face for the slightest hint of hesitation.

It was only when she thought she might simply dissolve with longing, beg him for mercy, that his mouth descended agonisingly slowly with a touch that sent heat whispering through her body.

This was not like the first kiss when the fuse had been lit by anger, a mindless response to recognition on some subliminal level that had set them both on fire.

Nor was it like the second time he'd kissed her. That had been a different kind of recognition, a shocked acknowledgement of mutual desire. It had been a kiss like the first one that would have had only one conclusion, but for the fact that she'd been thinking of another woman—a woman whom she imagined was waiting for just that moment.

This time, when he touched his lips to hers, he was not a male imprinting himself on her, staking a claim like some jungle beast. This was a man offering himself as a lover. Waiting to be accepted.

It was unexpected, enchanting, rare…and her lips opened in welcome.

Lucien responded with a slow, sensually devasting kiss that eliminated coherent thought and had her crumbling against him, wanting more, wanting everything.

'Honey…'

He eased away, looking at her for a moment, then there was clear air between.

'The bees are waiting,' he said.

'I've got a lot to tell them,' she said, unable to still the betraying shake in her voice. *A lot to ask them*.

'Have you got your phone?'

'It's in my pocket.'

'Call me if you need anything. And make a list of the jobs that you want done in the garden.'

'There's no need.'

'I'm the one in need, but you'll have to tell me what to do. You wouldn't want me pulling up precious weeds by mistake. What is the opposite of weeding? Flowering…?'

'You are being ridiculous.'

'Really? How wonderful. I thought I'd forgotten how.'

He kissed her again, a touch-and-go kiss, a promise that he'd be back, then he picked up her crutches and handed them to her. 'I'll do a couple of hours every evening. Fresh air, useful hands…'

And then she was watching his back as he walked away through the orchard.

'Lucien!'

'It's therapy,' he called back, not stopping, not turning round, and she didn't know what she'd have said if he had. 'I'll see you at five o'clock.'

'Wear work clothes!'

He raised a hand and then he was gone.

The first thing Lucien did when he arrived back at the Dower House, even before he'd showered, was to pick up the phone and call Jenny.

'Lucien…' He heard the uncertainty in her voice, a combination of relief that he'd called, but concern that he'd called. 'How are you?'

'Actually, I'm fine,' he said. 'Thanks for the emails. I'm sorry I haven't returned them.'

'I guessed you were busy with the book.'

'That's no excuse. How are you? How's Saffy?'

'Good. Blooming, in fact… She had her second

scan last week. All good, and you're the first to know that we're going to have a little girl.'

'That's wonderful news. I'm really happy for you.'

'Thanks. You sound…more yourself.'

'I've been getting out into the fresh air. Meeting the neighbours.'

'Oh?'

'I discovered that the nurse who stitched up my arm a couple of years ago lives next door.'

'The one you tried to find?'

'Isn't there a proverb about searching the world for something only to find it next door? In the prettiest thatched cottage.'

'Possibly…'

'She hammered on my door, accused me of murder and now—'

'Murder?'

'It's a long story.'

'Well, it's certainly bucked you up. You had an idea for a documentary about her, I seem to remember.'

'Not just her. Something much wider.'

'Is it still a goer?'

'It might link to the book.'

'Oh, well, that would be perfect. And it's wonderful to hear you sounding so positive.'

There was no mistaking her relief. She had obviously been worrying about him. Or maybe their partnership.

'We need to meet up and talk about what other projects you've got in the pipeline.'

'We've got a meeting with the accountants pencilled in for tomorrow. I thought I'd have to do it on my own, but if you could come up to London we could fit something in afterwards.'

It was too soon but, conscious that he'd left the heavy lifting to her for longer than either of them had intended, he agreed. Then, aware that she was now well into the countryside, he asked if she was familiar with re-wilding.

'Saffy has mentioned it.'

'Ask her if she's heard of a Professor Flora Rose.'

After that he called the village bookshop to ask if they had any of her books in stock. They did and Laura, the owner, offered to deliver them if he would rather not come into the village to collect them.

Then he had a shower.

The back door of the cottage was open when Lucien arrived a few minutes before five.

He tapped and called out, 'Honey?'

There was no reply, but when he went inside there was a note along with a photocopied map of the garden fixed to the fridge door.

The note said:

I'm down by the pond. H

The pond? Of course there would be a pond.

He dropped his backpack on a chair, put the curry in the fridge and took the map from the fridge door.

It was beautifully illustrated with little sketches of small creatures, flowers and insects, presumably for visitors to the garden.

He headed towards the far side of the orchard where the ground dipped into a hollow and, a few minutes later, spotted Honey on the far side of a large pond.

She was standing on a picturesque bridge spanning the small stream that trickled over boulders to feed the pond. Sandpaper in hand, totally focussed on rubbing down the hand rail, she hadn't noticed him.

Her hair was tied up and pinned to the top of her head and, as she bent with the push of the sandpaper, her dress gaped slightly, offering an enticing glimpse of curves that made his palms itch.

He stood very quietly, enjoying the intimacy of the moment. So much had changed since their first explosive encounter. Things had been said, there had been a world-changing kiss…

'Are you going to stand there and watch, Mr Grey?' she asked without looking up. 'Or have you come to work?'

He grinned. Some things had changed…

'Just admiring the view,' he replied, joining her

on the bridge. 'But I'm entirely at your disposal. Just tell me what you want, Honey.'

She glanced up, clearly about to come back with some quip, but no words came. As her gaze swept over his ancient T-shirt and lingered on his jeans, he felt his skin tighten. And she didn't have to say a word.

The answer was right there in her eyes.

CHAPTER ELEVEN

*'Next time a sunrise or a meadow of flowers
steals your breath, be silent and listen…'*
—Anonymous

HONEY SWALLOWED. Never had the bridge felt so small. Lucien was very close, and he wasn't looking at the water lilies or the flower-strewn meadow that rose along the valley, but at her.

'You'd like me to give everything a thorough rubdown?' he offered, and neither of them were under any illusion that he was talking about the handrails of the bridge.

'Um…' was the best she could manage through a throat that felt as if it were stuffed with hot rocks.

He took the sandpaper from her, dropped it in the work box at her side and took a step closer, leaving her in no doubt that do-it-yourself was the last thing on his mind.

'Lucien…' It could have been a protest or a plea—maybe it was a little of both. But even while her head was yelling at her to take a breath, take a step back and think about this, his T-shirt was bunched in her fists and her heart wanted him closer. To be touching him…

And then, blissfully, his hands were at her

waist, drawing her into his body, and she was lost in a slow, sensual kiss—a promise that Lucien Grey was a man who knew how to take his time. To give pleasure as well as receive it.

'Hang on,' he said, catching her behind the knees and sweeping her off her feet to carry her from the sunlit bridge into the shadows of the orchard. He put her down on the long, soft grass. She was still catching her breath as he stretched out beside her.

'What are you doing?'

Stupid question. Having unfastened the first of her buttons, he discovered that there was also a hook, and his fingers were tickling her breasts as he searched for it.

'I'm doing something practical with my hands. In the open air. As prescribed,' he said, looking up as the top finally surrendered. 'I can stop any time. Just say the word.'

He waited. And it was there. The word that would stop this so that they could go back to rubbing down the handrails on the bridge.

Her brain was holding it up like a red card at a football match, but it remained firmly stuck in her throat as her body, with every nerve end reaching for his touch, gave the referee the finger.

Two more buttons bit the dust with agonising slowness.

'What's this? No bra, Miss Rose?'

'Upstairs, out of reach. Get on with it, Mr Grey!'

Lucien obliged, parting more buttons, cupping a breast in his palm and holding it for a moment before brushing the tip of his thumb across a taut nipple.

Honey's entire body jolted as what felt like an electric shock reached parts of her body that hadn't been disturbed for a very long time and there was only one word hammering to escape.

'Yes!'

His mouth followed his thumb and for a moment she lay back, lost in the bliss of his tongue while his hand continued to work on the buttons until her dress fell apart and a rush of cool air on her belly woke her to the madness…

This had to stop. She had to tell him to stop. But the lace of her panties was no barrier and, as he touched the heart of her, she was clinging to him.

'Honey, sweetheart.' He kissed a tear away from her cheek. 'If this isn't what you want…'

Sensing that he was about to stop what he was doing, she grabbed his hand, holding it where it was, raising her hips to push hard against it and saying over and over what she wanted and couldn't have.

'We've no protection.' She slumped back to the ground, tears of frustration streaming down her face.

'Are you telling me that you didn't call the village shop the minute I left this morning and ask them to rush over an emergency pack of three?' He was looking at her with amusement now and she wanted to hit him. 'Are those the tears of a sexually frustrated woman?'

Her graphic response to that left him in no doubt how she was feeling.

'Hush… I've got you, Honey,' he whispered, his mouth at her ear. 'You'll find what you need in my back pocket.'

'You came prepared?'

'Would you rather I hadn't?' he asked, doing something indescribably wicked with the clever finger that left her nearly fainting with pleasure. 'Do you still want to do it yourself?'

'This morning, when I was sleeping like a baby in the grass, I was dreaming that I was naked and you were making love to me,' she told him, reaching for the button at his waist and making short work of his zip, her mouth promising heaven in a smile. 'All I want right now, Lucien Grey, is for you to make my dreams come true.'

'I'm sorry about the bridge,' Lucien said.

They had spent a long time over supper while she'd encouraged Lucien to talk. He'd told her about his mother and his childhood. At first, he'd been slow to yield the details of his childhood— how rejected he'd felt when his father had left—but he'd gradually opened up about school, university and the girls he'd known.

When they had reached the time when he'd begun reporting from the front line, he'd switched the questions to her, which was her cue to suggest they make a drink and take it outside.

Grateful that he'd taken the hint, Honey leaned back against the bench, stretching out limbs to which the life had been returned and looking up the stars.

'I'm not,' she said.

He laughed, recognising the words he'd said to her that morning.

'Nevertheless, I promised I would give you a hand in the garden.'

'And you totally delivered,' she said, smiling dreamily as she remembered every luscious moment. 'In the garden, in the shower, on the bed…'

'Honey?'

She turned to look at him, saw the question hovering, saw that he wanted her to tell him why she'd been alone for so long. But she was saved by Banks, who leapt onto the bench with a little growl then stepped onto Lucien's lap, where he began to turn around, plucking with his claws to make it more comfortable.

'What the…!'

Honey laughed, but mostly with relief. 'You're sitting in his seat, Lucien, so he's treating you as a cushion.'

'He's digging his claws in me,' he said help-lessly.

'He's making himself comfortable.' Banks, finally satisfied, settled down and began to purr. 'Congratulations. You've been accepted.'

'Only because our scent is now combined.'

Startled by this unexpected perceptiveness, she said, 'That will happen if you share a shower, use the same soap…'

'It's a lot more than that, Honey.'

His expression was so intense that she shivered a little at the enormity of what had happened to her.

'You're getting cold.'

It wasn't cold. It was a goose-walking-over-her-grave shiver.

Lucien lifted the cat. 'I'm sorry about this, Banks, but Honey needs to go inside.' He stood up and returned the cat to the warm place on the bench where he had been sitting, then offered Honey a hand up, putting his arm round her as they walked back to the cottage.

'Would you like me to stay, Honey?' he asked when they were inside.

Honey had no doubt that Lucien was sincere, wanting her to know that he wasn't a man to have his fun and run. But they had gone a long way very fast, and they were both a bit emotionally bent out of shape.

The sex had been hot, and perhaps they both needed that kind of physical distraction as part of the healing process. Sleeping together was something else. That moment when you first woke, before the barriers were up, left you totally defenceless...

'For some reason I'm bone-achingly tired,' she replied, 'and I have no doubt that you're desperate to pull another all-nighter on your book.'

'With no better offers...' He picked up his backpack and slung it over his shoulder. 'I feel the need to say something.'

'Goodnight?' she suggested before he did something crass like thanking her.

'Goodnight, Honeysuckle Rose.' His kiss was lingering, and she found it much too hard to pull away. 'It's been special. Dream some more, and I'll do my best to make them come true.'

'Go!' she said, laughing now. 'And no midnight dipping on the way home. It's dangerous to swim on your own at night.'

'You saw me?'

'I thought you were an otter.'

'What a disappointment.'

'No...'

It was ridiculous to blush, but she did.

Lucien laid his knuckles briefly against her warm cheek, then seconds later she heard the back door click shut.

* * *

Honey slept and she dreamed—tangled, mixed-up dreams filled with shadows and people who couldn't see her, didn't respond to her desperate cries. There were taps without water, endless empty corridors with locked doors and someone screaming in pain.

She woke in a panic, sweating and shivering, her throat raw, not knowing where she was. It took her a minute to fight her way through the fog and realise that she was in Flora's room, and that she had been the one screaming.

It was still dark but she rolled out of bed, afraid to go back to sleep, knowing from experience that it would start up again the minute she closed her eyes and stood for a long time under a hot shower, desperate to wash the nightmare away.

When the shaking had stopped, she put a fresh dressing on her foot. The simple task, done a thousand times, gave her back a sense of control. By the time she'd made tea and opened the back door, the sky was tinged with pink and the dawn chorus was in full throat.

It looked as if it was going to be another perfect day, but she checked the weather then clicked through her emails and texts. There were some from colleagues asking how she was, what she was doing. Quite a few from people in the village, urging her to call if she needed anything. The vicar, bless him, said that it was good to see that Lucien Grey was getting out and about and making himself useful.

She spluttered tea down her nose as she read that.

Useful!

The vicar's reason for texting was to add an autumn date for the wedding diary, which dealt with the laughter. September was a long way off and she didn't know where she'd be or what she'd be doing by then.

She'd never sell the cottage, but unless she could get a job locally she'd have to let it rather than leave it stand empty, and there was no guarantee that a tenant would allow strangers to have wedding pictures taken in their garden.

There was a text from Laura Wells, owner of the bookshop, inviting her to fill Flora's vacant seat in her pub quiz team. The chair of the WI was trying to fill her programme for the coming year and was asking if she'd consider giving a talk about her experiences nursing overseas.

A bleep warned her that she had a new text.

Did you dream, Honeysuckle Rose?

Nothing that I'd want you to make come true...

She thumbed in her reply, then stopped.
Lucien would be concerned, would want to

know what had been so bad, but she didn't want to think about her nightmare, let alone talk about it.

She deleted her response and instead typed:

I believe it's your turn to expose your fantasies.

Living dangerously, Honey? I have meetings in London today, but I have tomorrow marked down for bridge-painting and elderflower-picking. It's sausage casserole on the menu tonight, but I could mess with the system and swap it for prawns in a chilli sauce if you'd prefer?

Honey caught her breath as reality hit.

It wasn't the choice of supper that had her fingers curling back from the keypad. Anything that Alma had made would be a pleasure to eat.

It was the betraying heart-stop when Lucien's text had dropped into her inbox that stopped her from sending back a wicked text that would make him forget all about his meetings and come running…

She'd been sitting on the bench fooling herself that she was catching up on messages while in reality she had been waiting, like some desperate teenager, to hear from a man who had lit her up like Times Square.

The sexual tension had been off the scale three mornings ago when she'd been accusing him of murdering her butterflies. The sex had certainly been off the scale and she was fine with that. More than fine.

Great sex between two consenting adults was fun. Her friends and colleagues managed it and, even when things had gone wrong and they'd been hurt, they'd picked themselves up and got back in the game.

She'd had that once, as a student, but then she'd met Nicholas and it had just been the two of them, in a 'till death us do part' ring on her finger, 'see you in six months to plan the wedding', happy-ever-after relationship.

She'd waved him off at the airport six years ago and six days later he'd been dead.

She'd been in an emotional stasis ever since; all her energy, all her passion, focussed on her job. All her love had been reserved for the one remaining person in the world who'd always been there.

And then Flora was gone too, before she'd been able to get home to tell her all the things that she'd now never get to say...

The loss, the guilt, had ripped the heart out of her. She'd felt nothing but anger until a burning rage had sent her to Lucien's doorstep where, lost in his own world of hurt, he'd thawed her out with a kiss that for a while he hadn't remembered.

Then with kisses that she would never forget.

They both had huge gaps in their lives—family gone, jobs they loved but could no longer do.

It would be so easy to fill the void by falling into an emotional attachment.

But Lucien didn't need that kind of complication right now. The garden would help him heal. Talking, being with other people, a lot of great, uncomplicated sex… If she kept what they had light, physical, fun, she might be a conduit to his healing. But she had to keep it front and centre of her mind that this was going to be temporary. Casual. A summer fling that Lucien could walk away from, renewed, ready for the big life waiting for him once his book was written.

He'd asked her what she was going to do with her future. Next time he brought it up, she'd better have an answer.

She thumbed in her message quickly.

Have a good day but don't rush back. It's quiz night at the Hartford Arms so I'll be having supper there this evening—they do a very good steak with triple-cooked chips. If you fancy coming along and boosting the chances of the Butterfly Belles you'll be very welcome, but it's not compulsory.

She hit 'send' and then she texted Laura Wells to tell her that she'd be honoured to join the Belles.

Lucien read Honey's message, trying to read between the lines. She hadn't mentioned the quiz team. In fact, he'd had the distinct impression, from something Diana Markham had said that, like him, Honey had been avoiding the social life of the village.

He understood. She'd had some kind of breakdown and it took confidence to get back out there. But, despite their rocky start, she'd opened up the healing power of her home, of her garden, to him. Although it was her wit and her intelligence, and he'd be kidding himself if he didn't admit that it was also her sex appeal, that kept him going back for more.

Honey's demons were much harder to read. She'd opened up physically, no holds barred, and she'd talked about her grief at the loss of the aunt who'd raised her, but there was a lot more that she wasn't ready to share.

When they'd been lying in the orchard, drenched in the scent of crushed grass and the sharpness of some herb, catching their breath and laughing at the madness of what they'd just done, she'd let slip the words, 'I'd forgotten…'

Something in her voice, her words, had tugged at him. He'd reached for her hand as if to reassure her, though of what he couldn't have said, but the way she'd grasped it told him that his instincts had been right.

'Forgotten?' he'd prompted.

That catch in her voice had him braced for tears and her eyes had glittered over-brightly in the shadow of the trees. But she'd been smiling as she'd said, 'Excellent job on delivering the dream, Lucien. Can we do it again?'

He was hard just remembering that smile. Had been shallow enough to ignore the hovering question and missed the moment when, vulnerable, she might have let it all out...

This text was like that smile. A distraction. A step back from closeness, from the spilling out of secrets that followed an intensely intimate connection.

They had talked later over supper. Or rather, he had talked. She was a good listener, ever ready with a prompt.

Forget gardening. She would make a brilliant counsellor. And, like a good counsellor, she had kept it all about him. He should be feeling great about that. No emotional commitment, just great sex and counselling thrown in.

But he wanted more. He wanted her to trust him enough to share all her pain as he had shared his, having opened up to her in a way that he'd never done in counselling sessions.

She'd barely touched on the loss of her parents, of the man she had been going to marry, only opened up about her aunt. But it must have felt like a series of hammer blows. You got up from one and then there was another, and then the final one that tipped you over the edge...

He looked again at the text, shaking his head at

the inclusion of the team's name, Butterfly Belles. Was she hoping to frighten him off?

He regretted agreeing to meet Jenny today, but he couldn't let her down now.

While a night in a crowded bar held no appeal, it was good that Honey was getting out into the community, but she needed support. He called her and, before she could speak, said, 'You had me at steak, Honey. I'll pick you up at seven.'

CHAPTER TWELVE

'...nothing can bring back the hour
Of splendour in the grass...'
—William Wordsworth

HONEY FOUND HERSELF listening to nothing. Lucien, having delivered his message, cut the connection, leaving her quivering with a confused mixture of feelings.

The Hartford Arms would be packed on quiz night. His arrival would cause a stir and all those people he'd been avoiding would be there.

On the other hand, if she was on her own, she would be inundated with questions about him. His presence would take the pressure off her, and if he was prepared for that it could be a good outcome. If it went wrong...

That didn't bear thinking about. She considered texting Laura and asking her to warn everyone. But if everyone tiptoed around him, treating him like an invalid, he'd know and that would be far worse.

And she could be worrying about nothing. He might yet decide to drop her at the door and beat a hasty retreat. She wouldn't blame him if he did. She would certainly give him that option.

* * *

Honey was upstairs, still drying her hair, when she heard the four-by-four crunching over the gravel a few minutes before seven.

There was no time for anything fancy. She ran a brush through her hair, added a touch of lipstick to her face and then, hanging onto the handrail, hopped one-footed down the stairs, hoping to make it before Lucien discovered what she'd been up to.

Too late.

She had a split second to enjoy the knee-melting sight of his long legs in clinging jeans worn soft with age, a loose-fitting white linen shirt, the sleeves rolled up to the elbow exposing muscled forearms and his scar before he exploded.

'I leave you for one day…!'

'My aunt was a stylish lady, Lucien, but I needed my own underwear.'

'And you've painted the bridge,' he said, ignoring the chance to make some outrageous comment. He really was mad.

'Do you want to go and walk round the garden while you cool off, then come back and try that again?' Honey suggested, taking the last few steps and, when he didn't move, stepping into arms held out to catch her in case she stumbled.

'Dammit, Honey, I told you I'd do it.'

'I've saved the second coat for you,' she said,

putting a hand to his cheek where the stress lines were cutting deep. 'Did you have a bad day?'

He took a moment, a long breath, a shake of the head and then gave a smile of sorts. A contraction of the lines fanning out from his eyes softened his face and then moved to his mouth, slow, wide and heart-stoppingly seductive.

'Hello, Honey,' he said, and kissed her cheek. 'I love the way your sweater falls off your shoulder.' He kissed that too, taking his time until he reached the point where it curved into her neck. Then he kissed her other cheek. 'As for my day, I had to turn down lunch at The Ivy with my agent because I had a meeting with Jenny, the sandwich I bought had a severe case of depression—'

'That is rough.'

'And the train was running so slowly that I thought I would be late for our date.'

'This is a date?'

'I have to admit that it's been a while, but I've called to pick you up and take you out for the evening. What else would you call it?' he asked as he drew her closer, kissing her with sufficient ardour to demonstrate intention but with enough care not to mess her hair or smudge her lipstick.

She sighed a little, because it had been perfect. Too perfect.

'That level of flirtation is so practised that it deserves a slap,' she said.

'I'm glad that you appreciate the effort,' he replied with a grin.

She shook her head but was laughing as she reached for the crutches propped up at the bottom of the stairs. 'Don't feel you have to stop.'

'I meant it about the top. It's very sexy. But you're wearing a bra,' he said, running his finger under the strap in a way that sent a shiver ripping through her. 'And your skirt is too long. Those ankles were meant to be seen.'

'But not the technicolour bruises.' She lifted her skirt a few inches so that he could see.

'You're not wearing the brace?'

'My ankle needs movement, exercise,' she explained and, forcing herself to put a little distance between them, she headed for the door.

'I guess you know what you're doing.'

'I guess I do,' she agreed, swinging herself swiftly across the courtyard and leaving him to bang the door shut behind him.

'Even so. I'm sorry about today. It was stuff that I've been putting off for too long. That because of you I finally felt able to face.'

'I'm glad…' She paused to snap the seed heads off a couple of tulips. 'I put the first coat on the bridge because the forecast said there was the possibility of rain.'

He held out a hand and looked up at the clear blue sky. 'What forecast was that? The nearest we've been to rain for the last two weeks is some-where south of the Azores.'

'I might have been a little over-cautious,' she admitted. 'But with the wedding this weekend—'

'Wedding?' he repeated, startled out of his amusement at her inability to read a weather fore-cast.

Honey rolled her eyes. 'What is it about the wedding word that brings grown men out in a cold sweat?'

'I'm looking at you, Honey, and I promise you I'm not in the least bit cold. Are you sure you want to go to this quiz thing? It's not too late for prawns and an early night.'

Given the way that Lucien was looking at her, just getting to the car would be a win.

'I have to do this.' And she put on a sprint over the final few yards. 'Apart from anything else, I want to talk to the chair of the Parish Council about the state of the boat house.'

'The letting agent took some rousing to action. I was reduced to suggesting that you were consid-ering asking for damages.'

'But I was trespassing!'

'I told him you were visiting me,' he said, 'Which was true. You were. They are going to send a surveyor to take a look.'

'That is brilliant. Thank you.'

'I live to serve. Meanwhile, since the Butterfly Belles' need is clearly greater than mine...'

'You've had a rough day, what with the depressed sandwich and delayed train. You really don't have to do this, Lucien.'

'I've been in a pub before,' he said, opening the door for her. But his voice had lost that teasing note and a muscle tightened in his jaw.

'A pub where half the patrons want something from you? It's going to be noisy, and there will be no escape from the Diana Markhams of the village,' she warned. 'Just drop me off at the pub. I can get a lift home.'

'My face has appeared twice nightly in half the houses in the country, Honey,' he said. 'I'm used to total strangers acting as if they know me. But I'm not the only one here who's been avoiding the neighbours. And I'm not the only one in their sights. Your aunt's death has left a gap in the village and they're hoping that you are going to fill it.'

'Is that why you're tagging along? To run interference for me?'

'I'm tagging along because it's only the thought of spending the evening with you that has kept me going through the day.'

'That's a lovely thing to say, but next time take me with you. I can at least ensure your sandwich is edible.'

'I might take you up on that,' he said. 'But right now I'm going to pick you up and put you in the car, or we won't be going anywhere.'

She held up a hand to stop him. 'I've got this,' she said as, grabbing hold of the seat and boosting herself up with her good foot, she turned and dropped into the passenger seat.

'Spoilsport.'

'I'm attempting to dispel this notion you seem to have of me as a pathetic female who needs a man on hand to get her through the day.'

'I've seen you in tiger mode, protecting your infant caterpillars. You are many things, Honey—annoying, pig-headed, much too sexy for my peace of mind and the least pathetic woman I have ever met.'

He shut the door before she could think of a smart reply, and by the time he'd walked round the car and climbed into the seat beside her she was past it.

Lucien reached over and clicked open the glove box. 'I remembered that it's your birthday soon, although I don't know the date.'

'The tenth.'

'Well, if you look in there, you'll find an early present. It's not much, just a little something I saw in London that made me think of you.'

While he started the engine and pulled out into the lane Honey looked, and saw the iconic glossy green and gold gift bag in its depths.

'What is it?'

Scent? A silk scarf?

'None of the things that men buy women that

are always the wrong colour or a scent she'd never wear,' he said, almost as if he could read her mind. 'I bought practical gifts that you won't stick in a drawer and forget. Something that you'll use. Plus, a memory to keep.'

She loved a scarf no matter what the colour.

'Practical is good,' she assured him as she parted the green and gold tissue paper and discovered a pair of soft leather gardening gloves nestling in it.

'Lucien! They are perfect! And some truly luscious hand cream...' She looked at him. 'Are you hinting that my hands are a little rough?'

'No complaints from me,' he assured her, glancing at her then concentrating as he turned onto the road into the village. 'Keep looking.'

The bag felt very light, but further inspection produced a memory stick.

'I looked up the series your father was in, and called in a favour from a friend who transferred it onto digital from the master tape.'

'Lucien... I don't know what to say.'

'Wait until you've reached the bottom of the bag.'

'There's more?' She reached down into the bottom of the bag and, sure enough, found a package wrapped in green tissue and tied with a gold bow. 'What is this?'

'Reassurance.'

Puzzled, she pulled on the bow, unwrapped the

package and then gave a hoot of laughter as she found herself holding a box of condoms.

'Something practical that I'll use?'

'How and when is entirely up to you.'

'Thank you, Lucien. A precious memory and three very useful gifts,' she said, and then was overcome with the giggles.

'Well, I'm glad that was a hit.' She shook her head, unable to speak. 'Are you going to tell me about this wedding and what it's got to do with your bridge?'

It took her a moment to find a tissue and wipe her eyes. 'I'm sorry...' She made an effort to pull herself together. 'It's just something the vicar said about the fact that you were making yourself useful.'

'In your own time,' Lucien said when she lost it again.

She took several deep breaths. 'Okay. I've got it. Weddings... Village newlyweds come straight from the church to have photographs taken, in the orchard when the blossom is out, or on the bridge with the water lilies and the meadow behind them in the summer.'

'The water lilies... Of course. That was the clue.'

'It was?'

'The paint is the same colour as the bridge at Giverny. Nice touch.'

'If it works for Monet...'

'Maybe you should start offering the whole package,' he said. 'You're looking for a new career. "Weddings at Orchard End" has a nice ring to it. '

'No. This isn't a business, it's…' She stopped, wondering how she could explain it to a man who had lived his entire life in a city.

'It's a country thing?'

'More than that. It's a village thing. An Orchard End thing. Long before there were cameras, wedding celebrations took place in the Orchard End meadow. Everyone pitched in, brought food, someone played the fiddle, they danced, made love…'

'And more weddings followed as the night follows day. It's like something from *Cider with Rosie*.'

'We're in the right part of the country,' she pointed out. 'There's an old painting of a family wedding hanging in the study. His lordship provided a pig for the hog roast and a barrel of ale.'

'It sounds a lot more fun than any wedding I've ever been to.'

'Only if the sun is shining… Don't go in the car park,' she warned as they skirted the village green. 'Pull over here. If it all becomes a bit too much and we have to leave, you won't be blocked in.'

'I'll be fine,' he said, but did as she said and parked in the street.

'Ready?' he asked.

'Ready,' she confirmed. 'You?'

'Let's do it.'

It was a warm evening. The pub doors were fastened open and they could hear noise from beyond the bar door.

Honey was suddenly struck by a thought. 'Lucien…?'

About to push open the door, he said, 'Honey? Are you okay? There's still time to make a run for it.'

'Yes… No…' She waved away the suggestion. 'You were late getting back from town so how did you know I'd been painting the bridge? And that it's the same green as the bridge at Giverny?'

'Do you really want to know?'

She groaned. 'I've missed some paint, haven't I? Where is it?'

'Just here.'

He took his hand from the door and lifted a strand of her hair at the exact moment that the door was opened from the other side and they were caught standing so close that they might have been about to kiss.

The surge of noise that billowed out as the door was opened died away.

'Have you ever been in the Sunday papers, Honey?' Lucien murmured, his mouth close to her ear.

Her response, little more than breath, was scatological. Then, 'Do we run?' she asked. 'Or do we stay?'

'Lucien! How unexpected. How kind.'

Lucien lifted an apologetic eyebrow, then turned to face the woman who had greeted him.

'It's not entirely altruistic, Laura. Honey bribed me with the promise of a steak, but apparently I have to have to sing for my supper.'

'You're staying for the quiz?' She beamed. 'That's wonderful. Our table is just inside. I've forgotten my reading glasses, but I'll be right back. Honey will introduce you to everyone.'

The noise level had risen to normal and several people called out to Honey as they entered. But the Belles' table was near the door and there was no opportunity for people to detain her or engage them in conversation.

And no opportunity to ask Lucien how he knew Laura Wells before they were at their table and introductions had to be made.

'Lucien, this is Philly Wells, Laura's daughter, Josie Harper, who runs the post office, and Elaine Masters, who was one of Aunt Flora's oldest friends.'

'In every sense of the word,' Elaine said as he shook hands with everyone. 'I hope you're good on sport, Lucien, because this lot are useless, and I only know about motor sport, which never seems to come up.'

'I'll do my best,' he said, taking the menu that

Josie handed him and offering it to Honey. 'But no guarantees.'

'I'll have the rib-eye steak, medium rare,' she said without looking.

'Make that for two,' he said.

'And drinks?' Josie asked.

'Elderflower pressé for me,' Honey said. 'I'm on antibiotics.'

'And I'm driving, so I'll stick with water. Let me give you a hand, Josie.'

He started to rise but she put a hand on his shoulder, keeping him in his seat.

'There are at least three people lying in wait for you at the bar.'

'Maybe I should go and put Diana out of her misery now,' he said. 'If I agree to open the fete, we can all relax.'

'Oh, the sweet innocence of the man... Contemplate the words "inch" and "mile", Lucien, while Philly gives me a hand.'

'At least take my cash card.'

'No need. We run a table tab and divide the bill up equally at the end of the evening.'

Laura returned with her glasses and one of her shop's carrier bags, which she handed to Lucien. 'The last of the books you wanted arrived this afternoon. This saves me a trip.'

'Thanks, Laura.'

He handed the bag to Honey. 'Curiosity satisfied?' he murmured.

She put the bag at her feet without looking inside. 'Elaine was an international rally driver,' she said, curiosity under severe restraint.

Lucien, interested, asked all the right questions and Elaine, rising ninety, regaled them in her whisky voice with wicked, behind-the-scenes stories that had them all laughing until their food arrived.

The evening was relaxed and a lot more fun than she'd anticipated.

No one bothered Lucien while they were eating, other than a nod and, 'Good to see you here,' as they passed. Maybe Josie had issued a warning when she'd been at the bar. No one wanted to get on the wrong side of the woman who ran the village post office.

And the quiz was going pretty well, everyone head down and concentrating—the rivalry was intense.

And then someone dropped a tray of cutlery onto the flagstone floor.

CHAPTER THIRTEEN

*'Let me not pray to be sheltered from dangers,
but to be fearless in facing them.
Let me not beg for the stilling of my pain,
but for the heart to conquer it.'*
—Rabindranath Tagore

SOMEONE SHOUTED OUT a comment that made everyone laugh, adding to the noise and confusion, but Lucien was oblivious.

Before Honey could put out a hand to anchor him in place, he was on the floor, ducking, his arm held protectively over his head, knocking over his chair as he crawled for the door, desperate to escape.

His eyes were blank. He clearly had no idea where he was, only that he had to get away. Honey made a desperate bid to hold onto him, reassure him.

He shook her off and she clambered over the fallen chair to open the door so that he could escape. He saw the open front door ahead of him and he was on his feet and running before she could reach him.

He was fast, and too strong for her to restrain, even when she caught up with him. There was no hope of getting him into the car until he came out of it. All she could do was grab hold of a handful of shirt as he stumbled into the darkness of the village green, talking to him, saying his name over and over, spilling out a stream of the soothing words you would murmur to a distressed child. Telling him that he was safe.

Finally, he slowed, sank to his knees and fell sideways into a foetal position. They were far from the lights of the pub and the houses surrounding the green, out of sight in the middle of the cricket pitch. The grass was short, the ground hard and unforgiving, but Honey spooned herself around him as his body shook with sobs, holding him, keeping him safe, and all the time using soft, soothing words to bring him back from the nightmare.

Slowly he quietened and then, exhausted by the trauma, fell asleep.

Honey took a moment to text Laura and reassure her that they were both safe and that she'd settled up with her tomorrow. A little later, in the distance she could hear cars starting up and people calling out goodnight to one another, all no doubt wondering what had happened.

Tomorrow she'd call the chair of the WI and accept the invitation to talk about nursing in a war zone and the long-term damage to the men and women who had been under fire.

She felt Lucien stir and said his name, reassuring him that he was not alone.

'Where am I?' His voice was hoarse, cracked.

'You're safe, love. I'm here.'

'Honey…?' He looked around and when he saw her he groaned, pushing himself up into a sitting position. 'What happened?'

'You had a panic attack.'

He swore. 'I'm sorry. It hasn't been like that for a long time. If I'd thought for one moment…'

'No drama,' she said, quickly. 'But, if you're up to it, I think we should go home. Give me your keys. I'll drive.'

'I'll be fine.'

'They're not attached to your balls, Lucien. Give me your keys or I'll let your tyres down and we'll both be walking home.'

He looked, for a moment, as if he was going to argue, but then there was just the hint of a smile as he dug the keys out of his jeans pocket and handed them over. 'You don't mince your words, do you?'

'Parla come mangi…'

He frowned. 'Speak as you eat?'

'My last post was at a refugee camp on an island off the coast of Italy. It's what they say when you're struggling to get something off your chest.'

'Not something, I imagine, that's ever troubled you.'

'Or you, it would seem.'

'It's better to be straight,' he said, getting to his feet and offering her a hand, for which she was deeply grateful. While she'd been running she hadn't felt her ankle, but now it was throbbing painfully, and without his help she wasn't sure that she could stand.

'Let's go somewhere where the grass is more comfortable,' he said. She hung onto his arm, leaning against him, hoping that he'd think she was supporting him rather than the other way round. 'Did I make a scene?'

'Not much of one. You were out of there like a scalded rabbit while most people were looking at the poor girl who dropped the tray of cutlery. Don't worry. The Belles will have covered it.'

'I don't matter. I'm just sorry that I embarrassed you.'

'Believe me, I didn't have time to be embarrassed. The truth is that you'd had a long and tiring day in London.' She clicked the key to unlock the car door. 'If you hadn't distracted me, I would have noticed.'

'I wanted to be with you, Honey. I was having a good time.'

'I know, but we don't always know what's best for us,' she said. And she wasn't just talking about Lucien.

Despite not being fully recovered, he insisted on giving her a hand up into the driving seat, but she had to remind him to fasten his seat belt before she started the engine and took in a long, slow breath.

Her ankle was hurting like hell. It was a good job it was late and there were few cars on the road, because driving this thing was not going to be fun.

* * *

Elaine found her the following morning with her foot packed in ice.

'Josie said you looked rough,' she said, settling on the pouffe. 'But you look older than I feel.'

'I feel older than you look,' Honey admitted ruefully, but then Elaine drove a vintage sports car and had a partner thirty years younger than herself.

'How is your man? His car is parked in your courtyard, so I imagine he stayed here.'

Hadn't Josie mentioned it? The woman was discretion personified.

'I couldn't let him go home in that state and I've left him to sleep for as long as he can. Were there any comments after our somewhat abrupt departure?'

Stupid question. Of course there would have been comments...

'A couple of people asked if Lucien had been taken ill. I mentioned that he'd been to London and maybe he'd eaten something that disagreed with him.'

Honey laughed. 'He was complaining about a sandwich he bought for lunch but, seriously, thank you for covering for him. He's suffering from PTSD. The bombing...'

'I've seen it before, my dear. Back in the war, when it was called shell shock. And in drivers who've been in a crash. But what about you, Honey? You reacted too.'

'I jumped a bit, but then we all did.'

'British understatement is safe in your hands. Are you seeing anyone? You need to look after yourself.'

'I'm not suffering from PTSD, Elaine, but we've both been through similar experiences. Aunt Flora's death was the last straw, and I had a breakdown. I've had counselling, but mostly I'm soaking in the peace of the garden and drinking a lot of camomile tea.'

'That will help, but don't isolate yourself. I haven't bothered you, because it was obvious that you needed time to grieve, but I have been thinking about you.'

'That's what last night was about. Getting back into the community. I didn't intend to bring Lucien along, but he insisted.'

'He seems like a decent man.'

She told Elaine about the incident with the weedkiller—most of it—making her laugh. And the boat house. 'So, yes, he's a very good man. And now, by way of physical therapy, he's helping me out in the garden.'

Elaine raised an eyebrow. 'Is that what they're calling it these days?'

She didn't bother to deny it. 'It's nothing serious. He's just here for the summer while he writes it book.'

Casual…

'I'm glad to hear it. You need to get back on your feet and think about your future, but in the meantime a little fun is just what the doctor ordered.'

'Really? Who are you registered with?'

Elaine laughed. 'You're only young once. Make the most of it. But I wanted to see you to reassure you about Flora. You mustn't think that she was alone. She had her friends around her…someone was with her all the time, and she only allowed us to send for you because she knew you'd feel guilty if you weren't there.'

Honey swallowed down a lump in her throat and Elaine patted her arm.

'It was obvious how upset you were, and I was going to come and tell you how sorry we were that we didn't override her and call you sooner,' she said. 'But you were gone before any of us could catch our breath after the funeral. Obviously you were needed.'

'Yes…' Not a lie. Every hand was needed, but she should have stayed for a few more days. 'I need to see everyone. Thank them properly. Maybe we could have a memorial lunch?'

'She would approve of that. June—asparagus from my garden, trout from the river, strawberries and lashings of champagne,' she said, then laughed. 'Leave it to me.'

'That would be wonderful. And, Elaine, you

didn't leave it too late to call me. There were storms. I couldn't get off the island for three days.'

'It was an act of God, then. Out of our hands.' She nodded. 'The Parish Council will be in touch about putting a memorial on the village green. Steve Evans was all for commissioning some lump of stone with her name on it.' She rolled her eyes at the absurdity of the idea. 'Can you imagine what she would have thought of that?'

'I take it you shot the idea down in flames?'

'Not just me. Flora was growing oak trees from acorns she gathered in the Hartford woods. Brian has them safe and we're going to plant one of them on the green in her memory. With care it will provide a habitat for hundreds of living things until the next millennium.' She got to her feet. 'Is there anything I can do before I go?'

'Look in on Lucien? See if he's still asleep.'

Lucien emerged from sleep in slow stages, with an awareness of his face pressed into a pillow. Light filtering through sheer curtains. The sound of voices somewhere in the distance. He turned over and saw the space where someone had been sleeping beside him and then it began to come back to him.

Honey laughing. Laura bringing him a book. Eating, talking. The quiz…

His body jerked at the memory of the crash and, as he sat up, he realised that he was in Honey's bed.

He'd told her that he was going home but she'd driven him to the cottage, insisting that he shouldn't be alone. She'd put him in her bed and lain beside him, watching over him until he fell asleep.

He threw back the covers, and as he stood up the door opened.

'You're awake. Honey asked me to check.' The old lady was grinning and, realising that he was wearing nothing but his underwear, he pulled the bed cover around him.

'Where is she?'

'Lying down on the sofa with her ankle packed in ice.'

'Her ankle was better…' He knew he'd met this woman last night… 'Sorry, but I can't remember your name…'

'Don't apologise, young man. Not all war wounds are visible. I'm Elaine.'

'Elaine Masters. The rally driver,' he said, as that and a lot more came back to him.

'Honey took care of you last night, but she did more damage to her ankle when she ran after you, so if you're up to it she could do with a little TLC.'

'I'm on it.'

'Good. I hope to see you at the quiz next month. I'll make sure there's no more bother with the cutlery.'

'Maybe… Thank you, Elaine!' he called to her retreating back.

He looked round and found his grass-stained clothes where they'd fallen as he'd flung them off.

Or had he? As he picked up his shirt, he had a vague memory of Honey looking up at him, making some kind of joke as she unfastened the buttons.

It had been a while since he'd had such a bad incident. He sat on the edge of the bed, his head in his hands, trying to fill in the blanks before he had to face her.

All he could remember was the need to get away, running into the darkness and then Honey holding him… He'd felt as if he'd turned a corner in the last week here, in the garden with Honey. He'd sworn, after the break up with Charlotte, that he'd never hurt another woman. But he'd made a commitment to help Honey get the garden ready for the open day and now, because of him, her injury was worse. He had to fulfil that promise. That was the easy part. The hard part would be easing back from a relationship that had lit him up, given him a glimpse of a future.

But he had no right to inflict the mess in his head on her.

'Honey?'

Lucien, deliciously grass-stained and rumpled, appeared in the doorway.

'Elaine said you were awake. How are you feeling?' she asked. 'Do you have a headache?'

'Forget about me,' he said as he saw how swollen her ankle had become. 'I did that to you. I'm so sorry.'

Honey lowered the book she'd been reading, the one that he'd ordered from the bookshop about a re-wilding project in Scotland.

'I'm beginning to really hate that word,' she said.

'I know. It's meaningless, but you're in pain and I'm to blame.'

'No, dammit, you're not. If I hadn't decided to go to the quiz night, none of this would have happened.'

'And if I'd listened to you and stayed at home, you wouldn't be in pain.'

'I have pills for that. You're a more difficult case. Here's a test. Josie brought over some *pain au chocolat* this morning when she returned my stuff, so go through to the kitchen and have some breakfast.'

Instead of heading for the kitchen, he crossed to the sofa and folded himself up beside her.

'I haven't had an attack that bad for a while,' he said. 'But then I haven't been anywhere.'

'Failed!'

'I heard you, Honey, but you took care of me. Now it's my turn to take care of you. What can I do?'

He looked so desperate that she took pity on him.

'I suppose you could try kissing it better.'

'I'd love to,' he said after a barely discernible hesitation. 'But I haven't got a toothbrush with me.'

'I don't think my ankle will notice.'

'Kiss your *ankle*… Right… Got it…'

That he was not quite himself, that he had lost the sharp edge that always made their encounters so heart-poundingly edgy, was understandable. But that had sounded very like relief…

Even as the thought flickered across her mind, Lucien knelt at her feet and very gently kissed each of her bruised toes. He kissed the swollen, black and blue instep. Kissed her ankle so tenderly that Honey, who had foreseen breast-beating guilt and been determined to shrug it off as just a minor setback, closed her lids over the hot sting of threatened tears.

'Is it working?' he asked after a while. 'Honey?'

'Absolutely,' she said, blinking hard. 'It's the endorphins. They offer a temporary distraction from pain.'

'I can stay here all day if it will help,' he offered, but without the slow, thoughtful smile that never failed to send her imagination spinning.

'I have to admit that the idea of a man at my feet does have a certain appeal,' she said, making a determined effort to lighten the atmosphere. 'However, it would be hell on your knees, and there's a bride depending on you, so your future is breakfast followed by a couple of hours with a paintbrush.'

Lucien frowned. He'd no doubt anticipated being sent away to get on with his book, and had no doubt hoped for that escape, but the last thing he needed after last night was to be cooped up indoors reliving the events that had caused his problems in the first place.

'This is the outside-in-the-fresh-air, doing-something-practical-with-my-hands cure?' he asked.

'That's it,' she said, aware that he had avoided the word *useful*. And there had been no attempt to pick up her admittedly feeble attempt to raise a smile. Not that she was in any state for a repeat of their romp in the long grass.

He nodded. 'I'll see to it. What about you? Have you had anything to eat? Can I get you some coffee? Camomile tea?' Then he added without a hint of sarcasm, 'Can I carry you to the bathroom?'

'I've had a pastry and tea and a bathroom break, thanks to Josie, but you could take away the ice packs and put them back in the freezer.'

'She should have come and woken me.'

'She wanted to, but you needed the sleep more than I needed you fussing around me.'

'Fussing?'

Was that a touch of outrage? Better...

'Like a mother hen,' she said. 'And, while

you're clucking around asking me what I want, you're still failing the listening test.'

'Okay,' he conceded, hands raised in surrender as he got to his feet. 'What I need most is a shower and a change of clothes, but I'll take the pastry with me, and I will eat it.' He crossed a finger over his heart. 'I'll have to deal with the inevitable emails after yesterday's meetings, but then I'm all yours.'

'Better. I'll give you an hour,' she said, checking her watch as he gathered up the ice packs. It needed recharging. 'You'll find your keys on the kitchen table and the paint on a shelf in the stables. I wrapped the brushes in clingfilm when I finished yesterday, so you can use them as they are.'

'Yes, ma'am.'

'I'm afraid you're going to be on your own picking the elderflowers. I prepped everything yesterday,' she continued quickly before he could object. 'And this afternoon I'm going to introduce you to the art of making elderflower champagne.'

'You think you've got this all worked out, don't you?'

'If you don't think you can manage it, I'll send out a distress call.'

He shook his head. 'You are a piece of work.'

'And you are wasting your hour. You've already had three minutes.'

'I didn't think the clock started until I left.'

'Big mistake.'

'Seriously, Honey, you need to stay off your foot—and I don't care if that's "clucking".'

She smiled. 'No worries. I'll be the one lying back on an old cane lounger that's somewhere in the back of the stables. Behind the tractor. You'll be the one doing the work.'

Finally, a smile. 'I live to serve. Any special request for supper?'

'The sausage casserole will be perfect.' She looked at her watch. It wasn't showing anything, but she said, 'Five minutes.'

'I'm out of here Nurse Bossy Boots, but text me if you need anything before then.'

'You can count on it.'

Honey watched him as he walked away and heard the freezer door being opened and closed. She heard the clink of his keys as he picked them up. Small, everyday sounds, but the click of the back door as he shut it behind him had a finality about it.

He thought he'd blown it. It had been in every awkward move, every smile missed. This had been one setback, one bad incident, but he clearly believed that he was too messed up for even the most casual fling.

But, unless those birthday condoms were going to wither with age, she was going to have to convince him otherwise.

CHAPTER FOURTEEN

Take as many elderflower heads as you need, picked on a warm, sunny day, when they are fully open...

LUCIEN FOUND THE ancient cane chair, the kind of thing that might once have sat on the veranda of a rubber planter in the far east. He wiped off the cobwebs and added a couple of pillows, one for Honey's back and another for her foot.

A place had been created in one of the wide arms for a glass, and when the chair had first been used, it would probably have contained a glass of something exotic like a Singapore Sling. Today it was a useful home for her water bottle.

'Thanks, Lucien,' she said, easing herself into the pillow and allowing him to prop up her ankle. 'I haven't been in this room since Aunt Flora died, but cleaning it up yesterday, making it ready... I felt as if she was here with me.'

'And now?'

'Now it's mine, and I'm going to enjoy just sitting here, reading this lovely book you bought from Laura.'

But not nearly as much as she would have enjoyed being down in the meadow cutting the flowers herself, he knew. Although he didn't say that because she was trying desperately hard to prevent him from feeling guilty.

As if that were possible.

He picked up an oversized bucket and the secateurs. 'Fresh, frothy-looking blossoms from as high as I can reach,' he said, repeating his orders. 'And don't take more than a third from any one tree.'

'You've got it.'

'I won't be long.'

'Don't rush it, Lucien.' She smiled up at him and put a hand on his arm, and for a moment the temptation to lean in and kiss her almost overwhelmed him. 'Breathe in the warm air. Listen to the birds. Talk to the bees.'

'I seem to recall that they don't say much,' he said, forcing himself to move.

'But they listen,' she reminded him. 'Most of the time, that's enough.'

Honey watched Lucien go, aware that he was making a heroic effort to act as if nothing had changed, but the PTSD incident had undoubtedly shaken him.

Yesterday he would have kissed her before going off to forage.

Yesterday, they would have been doing it together. Laughing a lot. Maybe having their own *Cider with Rosie* moment...

Today, apart from being very tender with her

poorly foot, he hadn't touched her, for which she had no one to blame but herself. If she hadn't been running scared of feelings that were spiralling out of control, they would have been safely at home in her kitchen last night. In her bed, putting his reassuring and very useful gift to good use. They'd still have been putting up barriers against the outside world, but they would have been doing it together. Those barriers had come crashing down for her. The world had been beating a path to her door all morning, in person, on the phone and by email.

They had all been very tactful.

People were happy to see that she'd managed to bring their reclusive neighbour to the pub. No one had mentioned their early exit, or the fact that they must have seen that his car had still been parked by the green when they'd left at the end of the evening. She was just grateful that no one had come looking for them.

But the upshot was that she was now signed up for all the things she'd been avoiding since she arrived home. There was no way she was going to be allowed to slip back into hiding.

Lucien, however, might take it into his head to disappear, find somewhere remote and sink deeper into himself. Jenny had tried to help, but she'd had her hands full with the farm and filming, with a baby on the way.

It was down to her to keep him on station, and

she would do whatever it took to make that happen, even if it seriously annoyed him.

'Is that it?' Lucien asked.

The elderflowers were prepared for the champagne and were now weighted down, waiting for the magic to happen. The cordial was bottled and ready for the open day.

'The rest is time,' Honey said. 'I'll be okay by the time it's ready to be bottled, but thanks for today. I wouldn't have been able to do this without you.'

'I was glad to help. And it slipped my mind earlier, but Jenny asked if you'd mind sending her the recipe.'

Had he told Jenny about her?

'You could tell her yourself now that you're an expert,' she pointed out.

'I'd get the quantities wrong, and besides, you have the recipe on your phone. I'll send you her email.' He looked up from his phone. 'Unless it's some big family secret?'

'Hardly. She could find a recipe online, but of course I'll send her Aunt Flora's just as soon as I've had a bathroom break. If you'll give me a hand up...'

He took both her hands and held them while she got to her good foot and steadied herself.

They were so close. Lucien smelled of warm fresh air, the scent of blossom, the oranges and lemons he'd squeezed. So delicious that she could have eaten him by the spoonful.

For a moment while she found her balance, while he looked at her, the world seemed to stand still.

Then a shiver seemed to go through him and the spell was broken.

'Okay?' he asked.

'Fine,' she snapped as she let go of his support and grabbed her crutches. She was very far from okay. She wanted to scream with frustration, but instead she took a deep breath. 'Honestly… Just give me a bit of room.' He looked doubtful, but he took a step back. 'Will you make sure the windows and door are all fastened tight, or the sugar will attract insects.'

She didn't wait to see if he did as she asked but took off on her crutches. When she emerged from the bathroom, he was in the study, looking at the painting of the wedding in the meadow.

'Is your bride doing this?' he asked, glancing at her.

'I believe the wedding reception is being held in the castle, but thank you for reminding me that I need a path cut through the lawn so that she can arrive at the bridge without the hem of her very expensive dress turning green.'

'And that's my task for tomorrow?'

'Brian normally does it. Under other circumstances, I'd do it myself. If you think I'm taking advantage, please say.'

'I know exactly what you're doing, Honey, but of course I'll do it.'

'Great. That's a weight off my mind.' She turned to head for the sofa, then stopped. 'Did you happen to notice any dragonflies while you were painting the bridge? Metallic blue-green insects with two pairs of transparent wings?' she prompted when he didn't answer.

'I know what they are,' he said, a muscle in his jaw working overtime as his careful mask slipped a little. 'I wasn't looking at anything but the paint-work.'

'Could you do that tomorrow?' she asked. 'Count how many you see and maybe take a photograph? Flora kept a diary entry of these things, although she painted what she saw. That's one of her water colours,' she said, turning to a small watercolour sketch of a water vole on the river bank. 'And the garden map is all her work. I'd like to carry on with that for as long as I can.'

'Why?' He didn't wait for an answer. 'She had a passion for what she was doing but you're just going through the motions. Trying to do what you think your aunt would want.'

He turned from the watercolour. 'From everything I've heard about her, she'd be telling you to think hard about where you go from here—because if you are anything like her you're going to be doing it for the next sixty years.'

'Right now, all I can think about is getting through the summer. Doing what has to be done. Count the dragonflies, cut a path through the grass to the pond for a bride…'

Help a man she was falling stupidly in love with to find a way into the future.

'I'm sorry, Lucien. Forget it. You've done more than enough—'

'I thought the "sorry" word had been banned.'

'It's a "do as I say, not as I do" rule.'

'Why doesn't that surprise me?'

'Because I'm the neighbour from hell? The one that you don't have to pretend with,' she reminded him. 'But that's what you've been doing all day.'

'No…'

'Pretending you're okay when all you want to do is run back to the Dower House, pull down the shutters and refuse to answer your door. You don't have to run away from me. I understand what you're going through.'

'And you think you can cure me?'

'No, Lucien. Only you can do that. I doubt you'll ever be truly free of the panic attacks, but they will get less intense if you give yourself a chance.'

'And what about you, Honey? Have you been thinking about the hopes and dreams of your six-year-old self? It's time for you to stop dodging the question and think about what you're going to do for the rest of your life.'

'I can't remember. All I can remember is wanting my mother. It blocked out every other thing and that's the truth. So run away if you must,' she said, 'but don't bother about the ice pack. I'm going to take a nap.'

'Another one?'

'Excuse me?'

'You were asleep when I came back with the elderflowers. I could hear you from the courtyard.'

'Hear me?'

'Little piglet snorts,' he said. 'But then I don't imagine you had much sleep last night. Your ankle must have been agony.'

'I had pain killers.' She had them, but hadn't taken them, afraid that Lucien might wake up not knowing where he was and have another panic attack. 'But you're right. I didn't sleep until I was sure you were okay.'

'And I am, thanks to you. While I'm being an ungrateful jerk.'

'Just a bit,' she agreed.

'Dammit, Honey, you've seen what happens. I'm not fit to be with anyone right now.'

'We're both a little bent out of shape,' she said, lowering herself into an old and saggy sofa that had been in the study for as long as she could remember. She'd slept on it as a child while Flora had worked. 'Why don't you just tell me what's been eating a hole in you all day?'

'Parla come mangi?'

'Well remembered, but I can't talk to you if you're standing up.'

Lucien glanced at the leather chair in front of the desk, but she said, 'That's too far away. I want to see the whites of your eyes while you lie to me.'

He pulled the chair closer to the sofa and sat down in front of her. It jolted down to its lowest setting.

'You knew it would do that,' he said, glaring at her.

'It's old,' Honey said. 'And you're a lot heavier that Aunt Flora.'

'Okay, you've got me, but I'm not going to lie to you.'

'You've been doing it all day. Not consciously,' she said, 'but it's there in everything you do. You want to touch me, but you're keeping your distance. You want to stay, and at the same time believe you should leave.'

He didn't deny it.

'You said that you didn't have to pretend with me, because you didn't care if what you said hurt me—'

'Because I didn't know you,' he protested.

'And now you know me, it's okay?'

He swore, apologised, and swore again. Dragged

fingers through his hair as he sought the words to explain how he was feeling.

'Meeting you has been like a blast of fresh air blowing through my head, Honey. I thought I'd turned a corner but last night proved just how wrong I was. If we carry on with this, you are going to get hurt. Not like your ankle. I'm talking about the bits that never quite knit true.'

'Life is forever twisting us into something new. You've had a bad panic attack. They will happen, but if you take care of yourself they will become less frequent, less frightening. I'm not suffering from PTSD,' she said. 'I haven't been in a good way for a very long time, and it finally caught up with me, but things are getting better.'

'Fresh air and doing something practical with your hands?'

'It was helping,' she said. 'The only thing I lacked was the courage to put it to the test. Then your cowboy gardeners knocked down my nettles.'

'I owe them a drink for that.'

'For heaven's sake don't tell them why!'

'You think they'd be shocked?'

'I'm afraid they'd think it's okay to spray nettles.'

He laughed and she didn't think she'd ever heard a better sound. 'Heaven help them if they ever see you coming out of your corner fighting for something that can't defend itself.'

'It wasn't anger that saved me.'

She removed her watch, exposing the tattoo that the strap usually kept covered, and held her wrist out to him.

He took her hand. 'This is what jogged my memory that first evening,' he said. 'I remembered it from when you worked on my arm.'

She frowned. 'How? I was wearing gloves.'

'You'd finished with me and you were pulling them off when I looked back.' He ran his thumb over the tattoo. 'What are these flowers?'

'Forget-me-nots. They've self-seeded all over the garden. Little splashes of bright blue.' She turned her hand so that he could see the way it circled her wrist, then looked up. 'They are said to alleviate grief.'

'And do they?'

She shook her head and he folded her hand into his. 'Tell me about Nicholas. How did you meet?'

'Nicholas Furneval was a junior doctor. Six feet tall, a mass of light brown hair, green eyes. He was running along a corridor in answer to an emergency and, as he turned a corner, he sent me flying.'

'Don't tell me…he stopped to pick you up and got a mouthful of abuse for his pains.'

She laughed. 'You know me so well.'

'Well enough to know how that would go.'

'Not this time. He shouted an apology but didn't stop. He was waiting for me when I came off duty, insisted on taking me for a drink to apologise properly, which turned into dinner, then he insisted on walking me home, came in for coffee and never left.'

'You seem to have that effect.'

'You didn't stay.'

'You didn't want me to.'

'I was afraid,' she admitted. 'It was too fast.' Too everything. 'It's why I decided to go to the quiz night.'

'And why I insisted on joining you.'

'You knew?'

'It was the Butterfly Belles in your text. They were clearly meant to frighten me off.'

'You are too smart, Mr Grey.'

'I recognised the technique of a fellow bolter, Miss Rose.'

'I'm not bolting now, and neither should you.'

'No.' They just looked at one another until the clock chimed the hour and they both blinked. 'What happened, Honey? To your Nicholas. I know he died, but where, how?'

'Um…' It took her a moment to drag herself back to the story. 'He'd already applied to work for a medical charity and we'd only been together for a few months when he got the call.'

'He asked you to go with him?'

She shook her head. 'It was too late for that, but he produced a ring at the airport, said he wished I was going with him then went down on one knee in the airport terminal and asked me to marry him as soon as he came back. But he never did come back.'

'When was this?'

'He left London six years, eight months and three days ago. He died six days later, when the small plane in which he was travelling with a pilot and two nurses went down in a storm. It was in heavy forest, and they didn't find them for months.'

'So you decided to follow in his footsteps.'

'He'd wished I was going with him, Lucien. So I went. To be where he was. It was the only thing that made sense.'

He nodded. 'I can understand that.'

'Because you are a special kind of person. But I haven't told you this to make you feel sorry for me. I'm telling you because you think you're doing all the taking, and I want you know how much you've given me. It was finally making that physical connection. Feeling alive when you touched me.'

He frowned. 'There's been no one since Nicholas?'

'No.'

'You're beautiful, funny… What's the matter with the men out there?'

'Nothing. I was the problem. Some people react to loss with endless hook-ups, one-night stands, in an effort to recreate that feeling of being touched by someone you love. I turned inwards, because

I knew there would never be anyone else. I put all my passion into my work. That worked until Aunt Flora died.'

She was aware that Lucien was barely breathing, so afraid that she'd stop talking, but that wouldn't be right. He'd told her everything that had ever happened to him, and if they were to be partners in this he had a right to know why she was the way she was.

'I carried on for a few weeks but the guilt about not being there for her when she needed me, when she'd been there all my life, finally broke me. I was found raging at a frozen water pump. Kicking it, swearing at it, completely out of control. I had to be sedated before they could ship me back to London. I had a week in hospital, counselling sessions and then home to Lower Haughton where, like you, I had been avoiding all unnecessary contact. People put it down to grief and they gave me the space they thought I needed. And then your cowboys sprayed my nettles.'

He lifted her hand to his lips. He kissed the back of her fingers, kissed her palm, as if paying homage to her.

'What can I do for you, Honeysuckle Rose?'

'Nothing. I know I will never be quite whole again, not the way I was before Nicholas died. I'll never be able to love anyone the way I loved him, and I'm not looking for that kind of relationship.

But I can feel, I can laugh, Lucien. You've given me that. Given me back my life.'

'That's—'

'Too much responsibility. I know, and it's okay. This is just for the summer with no pressure to do anything but enjoy each other while we let the garden heal us.'

'And afterwards? What happens when the summer ends?'

'You have an important life waiting for you, Lucien. And while you were picking elderflowers I phoned Melchester University to ask about postgraduate courses. It's late, but Professor Flora Rose's name still has some pulling power. It may not be the answer, but I'm going to talk to someone there next week.'

'You make it sound so simple.'

'It is,' she said. 'Listen to the oak breathe, count the dragonflies, lie in the long grass and make love until the swallows depart. Then we can both start our new lives. No looking back.'

'Have you any idea what you'll do?'

'I'm interested in counselling,' she said.

'You'll be wonderful.'

'Thank you,' she said. 'And, now we've sorted that out, you can go and cut that path.'

He stood up but, instead of leaving, he joined her on the sofa. As the cushion sagged beneath him, she fell against him and he put his arm around her, drawing her closer so that her head was on his shoulder.

'That chair you were using today,' he said. 'The one in the still room.'

'What about it?'

'Can I put it in the glass house? If I put a plank across the arms for my laptop, I can write in there.'

'Is this because you feel obliged to stay and keep an eye on me?'

'Perhaps I want you to keep an eye on me.'

She turned to look at him. 'Maybe you should move in so that we can keep an eye on each other.'

'A *summer's lease*?'

'More Shakespeare?'

'He has the right quote for every occasion.'

'A no-commitment relationship with the end date pencilled in? A summer's lease,' she said. 'Although I should probably warn you that you won't be on your own in the glass house. I've an awful lot of plants to pot on for the open day.'

'I'll move the chair in later.'

'And now?'

'Now we'll just sit here and listen to the oak breathe. Maybe we'll fall asleep.' He turned to look at her with that slow smile that melted her bones. 'And maybe we won't.'

CHAPTER FIFTEEN

'The night is darkening round me,
The wild winds coldly blow;'
—Emily Brontë

IT WAS THE National Garden Open Day and Honey was at the pond with a group of children when her phone vibrated in her pocket. It was Alma, back from Spain with a fabulous tan and full of energy.

'Get back to the cottage asap! You have a very important visitor. Lucien is holding the fort, but he can't stay long—the visitor,' she added. 'You might want to run a comb through your hair.'

'What?' She had to be joking. At least one of the children always fell in the pond, usually on purpose, and she couldn't take her eyes off this bunch who were more of a handful than usual. 'Unless it's George Clooney, Lucien is on his own,' she said, just managing to grab the back of a boy's sweatshirt before he toppled in. 'What have you got there, Amil?'

He held up his jar to show her an eft but, as she gathered the children round to tell them about the life cycle of a newt, there was a scuffle and a small boy—one of the few who hadn't been hell-bent on a dip of his own—went in with a splash.

'Robert pushed me!' he yelled, floundering in

the water, his feet slipping on the muddy bottom as he tried to stand.

'Back!' she thundered, in a voice learned from a former sergeant major turned nurse she'd worked with.

Parents were supposed to remain close by, and some did grab hold of their offspring, but no one came forward to offer her a hand as she waded in and grabbed the boy.

'Pond dipping is more exciting than I imagined,' Lucien said, appearing exactly when needed.

'My hero. Can you take him?'

Lucien caught hold of the boy, getting thoroughly smeared with mud and water weeds as he delivered him into the safe hands of one of the helpers that he'd brought with him.

'I'm sorry I couldn't drop everything and come. Has the very important visitor left?' she asked.

'Not yet. Sir, may I introduce Professor Rose's niece, Miss Honeysuckle Rose?'

Sir...?

Honey threw Lucien a puzzled look and then turned to find herself face to face with royalty.

'I appear to have caught you at an awkward moment, Miss Rose,' he said, grinning broadly.

Standing knee-deep in the pond, and wondering whether she should curtsey, Honey thought the Prince had the situation pretty well nailed.

'Children and water...' she replied, deciding that it wasn't the moment for formality. Under normal circumstances she would have climbed out without assistance, but she wasn't about to risk slipping on the muddy bottom and going under, so held out a hand for assistance.

'Like iron filings to a magnet,' the Prince agreed as Lucien, who was trying very hard not to laugh, grasped it firmly. She gave him an *I'll talk to you later* look, then turned to her visitor.

'My apologies for not coming to meet you, Your Royal Highness,' she said, drying her hands on the hem of her T-shirt. 'But, as you can see, we've been pond-dipping.'

'Have you found anything interesting?'

'We have.' She looked around at the group of parents who were staring, open-mouthed. 'Amil, come and show His Highness your eft.'

Lucien brought Amil forward and the newt tadpole was admired while a dozen mobile phone cameras snapped frantically.

'My apologies for arriving without warning, Miss Rose, but I was a great admirer of both Professor Rose and her father. They were visionaries in their field, and when Lucien sent an invitation to the open day, I asked my staff to find half an hour when I could come and see the garden for myself.'

Lucien had done this…without warning her?

'You are very welcome, sir. I hope the WI ladies offered you tea?'

'They did, thank you. It gave Lucien a chance

to tell me what a special place this is. Not just the conservation and re-wilding work of your aunt, but about the healing atmosphere of Orchard End and how you have helped his recovery.'

'Not for the first time, sir,' Lucien said. 'Miss Rose is the nurse who took care of me when I was wounded.'

'You have known one another for a while, then.' He turned to her. 'Can I prevail upon you to give me the garden tour, Miss Rose?'

Nearly an hour later, their distinguished visitor, who'd seemed more interested in the healing aspect of the garden than the re-wilding, was ready to leave.

'Thank you so much, Miss Rose. Your aunt had such knowledge and vision. You must miss her a great deal.'

'Yes.' The word caught in her throat.

'The garden is delightful, but it's your experience with mental health that I'd like to tap into for a counselling scheme for young people that is being set up by a charity I am patron of. The way you're using nature to heal… My office will be in touch to arrange a meeting to discuss the role I have in mind.'

He didn't wait for a reply—obviously no one had ever said no to a personal invitation to meet him—but climbed behind the wheel of his car and, with his protection officer at his side, drove away.

'Lucien?' Honey said faintly.

'Yes?'

'Did His Royal Highness just offer me a job?'

'That's what it sounded like to me.'

'But he doesn't know me.'

'You are Miss Rose of Orchard End. Clearly that's enough.'

She shook her head. 'You're on first-name terms with him?'

'He's on first-name terms with me, which is not the same thing. We've met a couple of times at charity functions.'

'You knew him well enough to invite him to the open day.' She rounded on him. 'Did you know he was coming?'

'No idea, I promise!' he assured her, holding up his hands in surrender. 'Or I would have warned you. But he lives practically within shouting distance, and when I discovered that he'd written a foreword to your aunt's last book I wrote to him, hoping he might be able to spare half an hour to see Orchard End for himself.'

'Did he reply?'

'I had an acknowledgement from a member of his staff explaining that His Royal Highness had a very full diary and I assumed that was that. I was as surprised as you were when he walked in from the courtyard.'

'That must have given Brian a start. Did he ask him to pay the entrance fee?'

'I think the protection officer had that more

than covered. And Alma was brilliant, completely unfazed. You have stacked up a lifetime of Brownie points with her.'

'That's a relief. She's been a bit disapproving since she came back from Spain and discovered that you've more or less moved in here.'

'I think you'll find that's concern rather than disapproval.'

'Why? Has she said something?'

'She had a little chat with me about how much the people of this village care for you. A suggestion that hurting you would be a bad idea.' He grinned. 'There was just the barest whiff of the stocks…'

'Oh, Lord, I'm sorry. When you've gone, I'll tell her about our "summer's lease" agreement.'

'The whole line is "…and summer's lease hath all too short a date…" Did we decide which summer?'

'Lucien…'

'Alma didn't have to warn me, Honey. I know exactly how the people of Lower Haughton feel about you. I wanted to give something back, to show you and the village how much you mean to me.'

'A result, then,' she said quickly, afraid that this was going in a direction she couldn't handle, that he wanted more than she had offered, could deliver. 'Although, I would have preferred not to have been in mud up to my knees when he arrived.'

'I hadn't foreseen that possibility,' he admitted, 'but you can wear your best dungarees when you visit Highgrove.'

She elbowed him in the ribs then, relieved to have skirted a difficult conversation, and looked up. The afternoon had grown heavy and still, the sky had an ominous brassy tinge and there was a distant rumble that might have been a farm lorry passing at the end of the lane. Or might just be thunder.

'Did you hear that?'

'It's a long way off. It might pass.'

'I hope so. Once it gets trapped in the valley, it just goes round and round,' she said as a raindrop hit her cheek.

The rain was bucketing down by the time they'd got the tables and chairs under cover. Normally they'd take a walk, or sit outside for a while after supper, which would have been the perfect moment to talk to Honey about the future, to confess that he was falling in love with her and that he was looking for more than a short-term lease.

He'd tried earlier, but she'd shied away and he hadn't pressed it. Now she curled up on the sofa and pointed the remote at the television. 'Just checking the weather,' she said. 'Are you going to work this evening?'

'No, I'm going to sit here with you on the sofa and watch some rubbish television with you, just like an old married couple,' he said.

'Don't...'

'Honey, I know it's only been a few weeks, but I don't want it to end.'

'Please, Lucien. I've told you why that's not possible. What time are you leaving in the morning?'

He wanted to tell her to let go of the past, to give herself a chance and give him a chance to make her happy. But she'd shut him down, afraid to take that risk, and he took her hand and kissed it, wanting her to know that he understood her reticence to commit.

'I'm catching the seven-thirty-five train from Maybridge.'

'It's an early night, then.'

'An early night,' he agreed, taking what she was prepared to offer, prepared to wait for her to stop looking back and instead turn to face a new future.

Lucien stepped outside as the taxi crunched over the gravel. The path round the front porch was littered with pink petals and everything seemed to be sagging a little.

'The roses have taken a battering in the rain.' It had finally stopped some time around dawn, but the air was still heavy.

'We haven't seen the last of it,' Honey said, and he put down his laptop holdall and wrapped his arms around her.

'You said you'd come with me the next time I had to go to London.'

'I'm sorry, but you're going to be in meetings all day, and I can't leave Alma and Brian to clear up after the open day.' She cradled his face in her hands. 'Just stay away from coffee and alcohol, eat a proper lunch and, if it all gets too much, find a quiet spot to sit and breathe. Or you can call me any time.'

'I'll call you anyway. And I'll let you know what train I'm on.'

'Don't rush back. If your meetings drag on or you feel tired, stay in London.'

'I will,' he promised. 'If you'll promise to stay out of the garden today? Everything is soaking and your ankle is still weak. Read, knit, watch old movies…'

'No gardening. Got it. Now, go,' she said, picking up his bag and handing it to him. 'Or you'll miss your train.'

He kissed her again then, because he had no choice, he got into the taxi.

'Lovely old place,' the driver said as they set off. 'My mum and dad had their wedding party in the meadow.'

Honey, not a knitter and anxious about the weather, turned on the news at lunch time. There were yellow flood warnings in other parts of the county, but nothing for the Hart. Even so, she took a walk down the garden to take a look at the river. It was higher than usual and running fast, but nothing she hadn't seen before when there had been heavy rain.

Lucien rang. 'We've broken for lunch. How are things down there? There are flood warnings on the news.'

'That's further north. I walked down to the river and I've seen much worse.'

'Stay inside, Honey.'

'I don't knit. '

'Then read a book, play patience, cook short-bread. Please, sweetheart… I'll get back as soon as I can.'

'Calm down, Lucien. Everything is fine. Go and have something to eat. Do what you have to do, and I'll see you when I see you.'

'That's your bossy nurse voice.'

'And are you listening?'

'Okay, okay. Lunch, quiet place, breathe…'

There was a moment when neither of them said anything, because it was enough to hear one another breathe, then she heard someone call his name.

'I've got to go. I'll see you later.'

'Yes.'

After he'd hung up, she held the phone to

her breast, listening to the rain rattling like hail against the window.

She'd been so certain that her capacity for love had died along with her family, with Nicholas. Yesterday she'd stopped Lucien from saying anything that would change their relationship. But he'd made love to her with such heartbreaking tenderness last night and the thought of the autumn, just a few short weeks away, when Lucien would leave, was tearing a hole in her heart.

She hated that he was a hundred miles away in London, that she couldn't look in his eyes...read in them what he was feeling...

Half an hour later she received a text.

Baked sea bass, steamed baby new potatoes, broccoli with roast almonds for lunch, and a glass of delicious tap water. Now do you wish you'd come with me?

He'd said something like that before he'd left. *'You said you would come with me...'*

The words send a shiver through her, but she sent back a rude emoji, made a couple of phone calls and checked her emails. She discovered that there was already an invitation from an aide at Highgrove, with a document laying out plans for the mental health initiative and her possible role.

Excited at the prospect, she spent a couple of hours looking at mental health websites until, just after four, the sky went black, the thunder that had been rolling up and down the valley all day settled overhead and she lost the Internet.

She put on Aunt Flora's aged mac, donned rubber boots and went down for another look at the river. It was still within the banks but higher and running much faster, and low-hanging branches that had been torn off trees were being tossed around in the fast-flowing current.

She went inside and checked the weather warnings. There was localised flooding but no warning for Lower Haughton.

She called Steve Evans, the chair of the Parish Council and Chief Flood Warden.

'Steve, the river is running very high, and there's quite a bit of debris in the water.'

'I'm on it, Honey. We've set up a command centre in the pub and we're keeping a watch on the foot bridge in case of blockages. If you can keep an eye on the river level where you are, that will be really useful.'

She texted Lucien.

The weather is foul. The trains are going to be all over the place. Stay in London.

A minute later her phone rang. 'The trains are delayed so I've taken a car. We've just passed Maidenhead and the driver reckons I'll be home in a couple of hours. Go to the pub. You'll be safe there.'

'I will, as soon as I've checked the river level, but it's going to be really dangerous on the motorway after such a long dry spell,' she said, trying to keep calm and not say or do anything to cause him stress. The thunder and lightning would already be doing that. 'Pull off at the next exit and stay in an hotel.'

'Honey…' There was a crackle and the signal began to break up. 'I love you…'

What? No. He mustn't say that…

'Please, Lucien, get off the motorway. Stay safe!' she said, losing it, but the signal had gone.

Mind in a turmoil, her hands were shaking so much that she struggled to hit the call-back button, but when she finally managed it, it went straight to voicemail.

'Lucien, you remember how important it is to listen to me. I am telling you to get off the motorway and find somewhere safe.' Her voice was shaking as much as her hands. 'Please, dear man, do it for me.'

Do it because I love you too. I love you…

The three most dangerous words in the world. Words she couldn't say, shouldn't even think.

'Call me and tell me you've done that as soon as you get a signal.'

She switched on the drive-time programme on

the radio for the traffic news. There were accidents everywhere, delays, hold-ups…

She tried his number half a dozen times over the next three hours with the same result. Clearly he hadn't picked up her message or he'd be safe and dry in a hotel where he could have called her from a landline…

Unable to settle, she made constant trips to the river. The low cloud cover and constant rain meant that it was dark much earlier than usual. By seven o'clock, using the torch on her phone, she could see that water was spilling over the bank.

She called Steve.

'There's a report of a blockage at the footbridge. It looks as if someone's shed has been washed away. It must have been pretty substantial, or it would have broken up, but everything is catching on it. A team is on its way to clear it now.'

'It could be the boat house. I'm going to check.'

'Be careful, Honey. Don't take any risks.'

The continuous lightning followed by cracks of thunder was like a night-time rocket attack and it took all of Lucien's concentration and careful breathing to remain focussed on where he was. On Honey. His need to know that she was safe.

It got worse as he neared Lower Haughton after delays caused by accidents, breakdowns and endless detours. It had been nearly five hours since he'd been able to get a signal.

It was lashing with rain when they finally drew up outside The Hartford Arms. Inside it was buzzing with activity but he could see at a glance that Honey wasn't there.

'Lucien…' Josie looked up from filling a flask with soup. 'Thank goodness. Honey's been frantic with worry.'

'I couldn't get a signal. A lightning strike somewhere… Where is she?'

'Monitoring the river level.'

Of course she was.

'I'll send my driver back. His name's Marek and he's been an absolute hero. He needs food and a bed for the night.' He took out his wallet, offering a card.

'I'll sort it. You can settle up later. Go and find Honey.'

Ten minutes later they were at the cottage. 'Go back to the pub, Marek. Call your family to let them know you're safe. Josie will take care of you.'

He checked the cottage, desperately hoping that Honey would be safe in the warm and dry. As if…

The light was on in the kitchen, but there was no one home. He dumped his laptop bag and ran down the garden towards the river. He was ten metres from the gate when water began to fill his shoes.

'Honey!'

He'd hoped to find her by the gate, but there

was a glow of light and noise from further along the path in the direction of the boat house.

A lurching sense of dread sent him racing through water over his ankles. Rounding the bend, he could see that one of the supporting pillars had given way, that what was left of the deck was slewed at a drunken angle, half in the water.

He sought out Honey amongst shadowy figures working under an arc light to free the deck from the remaining support so that it could be winched out of the water.

'Honey!' His shout was blown away by the wind, drowned out by the whining of a chain saw and the continuous rumble of thunder.

And then she was there, her pale hair blowing about her face as she moved closer to the light, completely absorbed in thumbing a message into her phone.

'Honey!' he called again, just as a flash of lightning, so close that his hair crackled with static, struck the boat house, sending up a volley of sparks and freezing the scene so that it seemed as if he was the only one still moving, running through treacle as he heard an ominous ripping that overrode every other noise. Although he was shouting, it was like a nightmare where there was no sound.

And then he was diving towards her as the balcony parted company with the upper floor of the boat house.

CHAPTER SIXTEEN

'I sing of brooks, of blossoms, birds, and bowers;
Of April, May, of June, and July flowers.
I sing of May-poles, Hock-carts, wassails, wakes,
Of bride-grooms, brides, and of their bridal cakes.'
—Robert Herrick

HONEY HIT THE ground with a thump that shook her bones. For a moment she just lay there, winded, trying to work out what had happened.

The light had gone out, there was a smell of burning and someone was lying on top of her. For a moment it was as if a bomb had gone off, but she was lying in mud, and someone was flashing a torch in her direction and she saw Lucien's face beside her. Blood, mingled with rain and mud, was running from his temple and he was utterly still.

Someone shouted, 'Paramedic!'

The next few minutes were like something out of a nightmare as she lay there while they tried to assess exactly what the situation was.

A groan reassured them and then Lucien opened his eyes.

'You were right about the motorway,' he muttered. 'Bad decision.' And then he closed them again.

'Is he making sense, miss?'

'Yes…' The word stuck in her throat.

'Can you tell me exactly what happened?' the paramedic asked once they'd got him into the ambulance.

'He saved my life.'

Lucien had been unconscious for what felt like the longest couple of minutes in her life.

The paramedic smiled at her, but didn't pause in his practised attachment of electrodes to Lucien's chest. 'I was thinking more about how Mr Grey was injured. No one else was near enough to see exactly what happened.'

She shook her head. 'He came out of nowhere and pushed me clear…' She'd heard a shout, had a momentary glimpse of the balcony disintegrating and pieces falling and then he'd barrelled into her, knocking her clear…

'It's looks as if something caught him on the side of the head.'

'A piece of wood.' She wanted to push the paramedic aside and examine him herself. 'Is there a depression in his skull?'

'I'll leave the poking about to the doctors. They'll stick him in the scanner and that will tell them everything they need to know.'

'I thought he was dead. He could have died…' She looked at Lucien, lying on the gurney in the ambulance, the whiteness of his face accentuated by a smear of blood from a cut on his forehead. His neck was in a brace…

'He's had a knock on the head but his breathing and blood pressure are okay. Just as well someone had the foresight to ask for an ambulance to be on standby.'

'Ambulance, fire service with a winch… I should be there. I'm supposed to be sending back reports to the flood warden.'

A hand grabbed her arm. 'You are going nowhere.'

'Don't move!' she said as Lucien tried to sit up.

He groaned, and lifted his hand to his head. 'I feel as if I've been hit by a truck. What happened?'

'You were playing the damn hero as usual,' she said, leaning over him so that he could see her.

'You're hurt!'

'No.' Just scared witless that his mad act of bravery had come close to killing him.

'Your face… Sweetheart, you're bleeding…'

'It's nothing. A scratch where I hit the ground. I'm not hurt, and neither would you have been if you'd listened to me and stayed in London.'

'Failed again. You'll have to write "must try harder" on my end-of-term report.'

'Idiot!' But she put a hand to her mouth and shook her head. She'd been determined to remain professional, calm. How dared he lie there, the colour of chalk, and make a joke of it? She'd so nearly lost him. Might still lose him…

'Don't cry, Honey.' His hand slipped down her arm to take her hand. 'It's not every day a man gets to save the life of the woman he loves.'

'They're not tears. It's raining…'

'And I'm Dick Robinson.'

'Then it's time to change your name by deed poll,' she said, smearing the tears and blood away with her palms.

'Mrs Grey or Mrs Robinson…' He caught his breath. 'Your choice.'

'Don't!'

'What?'

'You scarcely know me.'

'I knew you from that first moment, and if that bomb hadn't hit…' He stopped for a moment. 'I've been searching for you ever since, Honey. I just didn't know it. I love you, Honeysuckle Rose—'

'No.' She'd been shaking ever since he'd swept her from under the path of the balcony, but now her legs gave way and she sat down very suddenly. 'Don't! Don't say that.'

'That I love you?'

'You were so still… I thought you were d-dead, and it would have been my fault. If I'd done what you asked and gone to the pub…'

'You wouldn't have been my Honeysuckle Rose. Protector of caterpillars, healer of broken souls…'

The paramedic frowned, clearly concerned that he was rambling.

'We're ready to leave, Honey, so you need to be strapped in. '

She didn't want to take her eyes off Lucien, desperately afraid that he might have a fractured skull, that even now pressure might be building in his brain, that he'd slip into a coma and never wake up. Because that was what happened to the people she loved. They died.

But the ambulance couldn't move until she was properly seated, and she turned to face the front, fastening herself in while the ambulance doors were secured. Focussing on steady beats from the monitor, listening for the slightest warning of collapse.

The paramedic made some notes then looked up. 'Are you all right, miss? You've had a shock. Let me check your blood pressure.'

She was shaking and her teeth were chattering, but she surrendered her arm without argument, allowing nothing to distract her from Lucien.

'A bit low. Not surprising after such a shock. I'll mention it when we get to the hospital,' he said, offering her a box of tissues and a bottle of water.

'The rain,' he said kindly. 'It's run through the mud.'

'What? Oh, yes, the rain.' She mopped her face. 'Thank you.'

'He'll be okay.'

She wanted to tell him that she was a nurse and knew every possible outcome of a head trauma. How sometimes someone who seemed beyond saving made a recovery against all the odds. How sometimes what seemed to be a minor injury felled the strongest man.

But he was being kind, so she forced a smile and kept listening to the monitor.

Lucien woke with a splitting head, limbs that felt like lead and a moment of blinding panic when he was fighting to get away and escape before the familiar monotonous beeps and the unmistakable hospital smell brought the night rushing back in all its horror.

The rain, the river, the boat house and Honey...

'Honey!'

'Lo, the hero wakes.'

He turned. 'Jenny? What the hell are you doing here?'

'Hello, Jenny, how kind of you to drop everything and drive through storm and flood to bring me comfort. Are those grapes?' She plucked one from a bunch on the night stand. 'Just what the doctor ordered,' she said, popping it into her mouth.

'Where's Honey?' he asked, ignoring her sarcasm. 'How is she?'

'She was on the far side of stressed last night when she called me, demanding that I get here "though hell should bar the way". Or perhaps that's her normal state?'

'Not even close. She didn't actually say that?'

'Quote Noyes? She might as well have. If that's not her usual state of mind, I'll put it down to her brush with the Grim Reaper. Or maybe it was your close call that reduced her to a gibbering wreck.'

'For pity's sake…'

'Sorry, but it's hard not to tease a man so completely in the throes. I have to admit that she did look pretty grim. Mud, dried blood—that might have been yours—and a face whiter than the cliffs at Dover. The doc pulled up her records and, once I arrived to keep watch, she let him give her a sedative and find her a bed.'

'Where is she?' he demanded, tossing aside the blanket.

'Whoa! That gown is way too short!'

He pulled the blanket off the bed, tucked it round him and disconnected the drip attached to his arm.

'You're going to get into so much trouble with Sister,' she warned as the bleeping went into overdrive. 'Although, since the hospital is buzzing with rumours that you asked Honey to marry you in the ambulance—so romantic, but sadly too late to make today's headline—I guess you already are.'

'Mr Grey! What do you think you're doing?' Sister demanded, coming into the room.

'I'm going to find the woman I love.'

'Miss Rose is asleep.'

'Then I'll sit by her bed until she wakes up and answers my question. Or I could just discharge myself!'

'I'd listen to him,' Jenny advised. 'He's not in a joking mood.'

'He's had a bang on the head. That will knock the humour out of most people.'

'What's the damage?' Jenny asked.

'I believe the radiographer was overheard to say that he'd never seen a harder head. The doctor will be round to see you in an hour or so, and he'll probably discharge you if you've got someone to keep an eye on you.' Sister looked at Jenny. 'Would that be you?'

'No, it's not,' Lucien said before she could answer.

'Are you sure? It's the reason Honey summoned me,' she said. 'She wants me to take you home with me.'

'I am home.'

'Then I'll get back to my sheep.' She gave him a hug. 'Take care, partner. The network said yes to the idea you pitched to them yesterday, so you're going to have your hands full.'

'I'm fine.'

'Go and find your Honey, foolish man. And let me know if she says yes. I'll need to go hat shopping.'

Honey ached, her mouth was dry and she had to force her gritty eyes to open. It took a moment for her brain to catch up with the curtains around her bed and remember where she was.

Instantly awake, alert, she flung back the bed-clothes. 'Lucien...'

'Here, miss.'

She swung round and, as if she'd conjured him up, there he was, wrapped in a blanket and sitting in the chair beside her.

'What on earth are you doing here? You should be in bed!'

'Absolutely.' He stood up. 'Move over. You look in need desperate need of a hug.'

'What? Lucien, you can't!' But he eased himself in beside her and pulled up the covers.

'A bit snug,' he said, putting his arm around her. 'Turn on your side and hang onto to me, or I might fall out and hurt myself.'

'You'll get us thrown out,' she said, but shifted onto her side so that she was pressed up against him, her head on his shoulder, her hand against his heart.

'Checking it's still ticking?'

She started, and pulled back, but he caught her hand and held it there.

'I thought you were dead. Then I was afraid you'd die because that's what happens to the people I love.'

'I know, sweetheart. While I've been sitting here, waiting for you to wake up, I've worked it out.'

'I don't know what you're talking about.'

'Yes, you do. You change the subject whenever the word "love" gets mentioned.'

'I can't…'

'You can't say it, Honey, but never tell me that you don't feel it.' Her hair was stiff with dried mud but he kissed the top of her head. 'Don't cry, sweetheart. It doesn't matter. They are just words.'

'I'm not crying,' she said, ignoring the hot tears running down her cheeks and into his gown. 'I never cry.'

'It's going to be Mrs Robinson, then.'

She shook her head and pulled away. 'It's not a joke,' she said. 'You think you understand, but you don't. Those three words have been the last thing I've said to everyone I've ever loved. My parents, Nicholas, Aunt Flora…'

'Your parents? You were only six years old.'

'I didn't understand why they were going away without me. I thought I'd done something wrong, and I ran down the drive, chasing the car, shouting, "I'm sorry, I love you", hoping that they'd hear and come back for me.'

'But they never did,' he said, thumbing the tears from her cheeks. Then he drew her close so that her face was pressed into his neck and the comfort of his steady pulse.

'I told you that they died in a traffic accident, but it was a motorway pile-up in bad weather. Twenty-odd cars, half a dozen fatalities.'

'I'm so sorry. If I'd known... And days after you saw him off, no doubt saying those same words, Nicholas died in a plane crash. I can see why you'd link the two incidents in your mind.'

'And the last time I saw Aunt Flora she said the kind of things you'd say to someone you don't expect to see again.'

'She was ninety-four...'

'I thought she'd last for ever, that we'd celebrate her one hundredth birthday with a party on the village green. But she knew she wouldn't see me again, and if I'd been paying attention I'd have known too. But I was busy packing, my head full of where I was going, what I'd need...'

He hitched himself onto his side so that he was facing her. 'Look at me, Honey.'

She lifted her gaze from his neck.

'She said everything she wanted you to know. You respect her best by living your best life and paying that love forward.' He wrapped his arms around her. 'You told me that I'd given you back your life. In the vanishingly small possibility that I get wiped out by a freak accident, do you really want to waste a minute of whatever time we have running from the risk that I might not survive until I'm ninety-four?'

'Ninety-four?'

'At a conservative estimate.' He waited. 'Unless, having got your life back, you're all set to start swiping right and making up for lost time?'

She didn't answer.

'Honey?'

'I'm thinking about it,' she said.

'I guess I deserve that.'

'I guess you do.'

'I'll make it easy for you. I don't want you to love me the way you loved Nicholas. I want you to love me because I'm someone who knows you and loves you for the woman you are now. And that's the last time I'll say it. Forget the words. They can join "sorry" in the "banned" dustbin. Love is what you do, not some empty phrase on a million Valentine cards.'

'Okay.'

'Is that your answer?'

She lifted her face from his chest and looked at him. 'To the Mrs Grey or Mrs Robinson question?'

'That's the one.'

'That's a lot bigger than the online dating question. Lucien, I need longer to think about it. Ask me again when you open the fete.'

* * *

Lower Haughton was packed for the annual summer fete. Everywhere was decorated with bunting. There were stalls selling everything, fairground rides, a 'scruffiest dog' show, pony rides. Rosie, the ice-cream van which appeared in a television soap opera filmed in Upper Haughton was there, and so was Honey, sitting at the wheel of her tractor and trailer.

The vicar tapped the microphone, deafening everyone. Certain that it was working, he said, 'Good afternoon, ladies and gentlemen. Welcome to the Lower Haughton Summer Fete. It's been a difficult few weeks but, thanks to the heroic efforts of everyone involved in clearing the river of the debris from the boat house, floods didn't reach the village. The footbridge was badly damaged, but the good news is that the Hartford estate have agreed to pay for the repairs. So the money raised today will go towards essential repairs for the village hall.'

A cheer went up from the crowd.

'I'm glad you all approve. But now, since I know that you're all itching to get out there and spend your money, I'm going to hand you over to Mr Lucien Grey, who you will all know from his news broadcasts from trouble spots and his own heroic efforts in rescuing civilians from their bombed house at Bouba al-Asad. And who saved our Honey...'

Lucien stepped up to the mike and waited for the applause to die down.

'A hero,' he began, 'is not someone out of the ordinary or gifted with special powers. A hero is a man or woman who, faced with a difficult situation, steps up and does what's necessary.

'There are heroes in this valley, in this village,' he went on. 'Men and women who manned phones, who risked their lives in appalling conditions to save their neighbours, their friends and their loved ones from threatened floods.'

He looked across the green to where Honey was sitting on her tractor, her hair tied up in a scarf nineteen-forties-style, wearing the same dungarees as she had the day she'd arrived at his door.

'There is one woman here,' he continued, 'who has risked her life many times for strangers—people who she will see for a few minutes, maybe an hour at the most, working in intolerable conditions. You all know Honeysuckle Rose.'

Another cheer went up, and applause.

Honey shook her head, but she'd asked for this.

'I came to Lower Haughton seeking refuge, a place to deal with the kind of wounds that are not visible. But Honey saw them, saw me, and made me part of this community. And if Miss Honeysuckle Rose will do me the enormous honour of marrying me, this is going to be my forever home.'

He looked across the green, where the heads of the expectant crowd faced her, and it was as if it was just the two of them as he said, 'Honey? What's it to be?'

As one, the entire crowd turned to look at her, holding its breath.

And Honey—after the kind of pause more usually associated with announcing the winner of television baking show—tugged on a rope and unfurled a banner above her head that read: *The future Mrs Grey*.

A huge cheer went up from the crowd. Honey was off the tractor and Lucien was off the podium and they were racing towards each other.

The crowd parted for them, clapping and chanting, 'Kiss, kiss, kiss…!' And then she was there in front of him, and she was in his arms, and he was kissing her. Everything in his world was about as right as it could be.

She pulled back, laughing. 'Nicely done, Mr Grey, but you still haven't opened the fete.'

'I declare this fete open!' he shouted.

More cheers then, having seen the show, everyone moved off to enjoy the fun, leaving them alone.

'I have something for you,' he said, producing a small velvet box and opening it to reveal a rather spectacular half-hoop of diamonds. 'Not useful this time, but it is for ever.'

* * *

Honey and Lucien's wedding day began on a fine day in early September with a simple ceremony in a quiet corner of the village green, where all Flora's friends had gathered to plant an oak sapling in her memory.

Later, they made their vows in the age-old ceremony in the church, paused for photographs on the bridge and then the meadow was the venue for the kind of old-fashioned wedding party that Honey's great-grandfather would have recognised.

There was a marquee for the buffet, a dance floor laid down on the turf for dancing and a traditional hog roast for the evening, when all the guests sat out under the stars. There was a barrel of ale from the local brewery, elderflower cordial for the children and champagne for the adults, which all the village women had pitched in to make.

There was a fiddler and a local rock group for the dancing, and it was the group that was going to play for their first dance.

Lucien took Honey by the hand and they stood there for a moment, smiling at one another, barely able to believe how lucky they were to have found each other.

They hadn't had to think twice about the song they'd chosen. It wasn't something smoochy. They hadn't had that kind of relationship. It was a song to remind them of special moments, something to make them laugh.

'Shall we dance, Mrs Robinson…?' Lucien invited, 'Shall we dance, Mrs Robinson…' as the two guitarists in the band launched into the song, and he began to spin her into their new life together.

* * * * *

If you enjoyed this story,
check out these other great reads from
Liz Fielding

Her Pregnancy Bombshell
The Billionaire's Convenient Bride
A Secret, a Safari, a Second Chance
Christmas Reunion in Paris

All available now!